# ARGOSY
# VOLUME 2:

# PULP
# MODERN

# ARGOSY
## VOLUME 2:

# PULP
# MODERN

Edited by Daniel Bazinga

# CONTENTS

# THE BEAT OF HEAVY WINGS

*by Kurt Newton*

**1.**

Barry was my older brother. Three years older. I didn't know that the first night we went moth hunting out in the woods would be our last.

"C'mon, Drew, it's almost dark!"

"I'm coming ... Jeez..."

Up ahead, Barry carried a Coleman lantern, butterfly net, and a five-gallon bucket. The sheet, hammer and nails, some baling wire, and a flashlight were stuffed in the bucket. I carried another five-gallon bucket full of his collection kits. I also wore a backpack jammed with sodas and snacks. I remember one of the soda cans kept digging into my ribs as I walked.

"Drew, I mean it. I want to set this thing up while we can still see."

"Can't we just use the flashlight?"

"Don't be stupid. Why waste the batteries if we don't have to? C'mon—God, you're so slow."

I could see Barry shaking his head. For a younger brother I must have been a big disappointment. Barry was tall and thin. I was shorter than most boys my age and, at ten years old, just wasn't as strong or as fast. I did my best to keep up, but sometimes that wasn't good enough.

"We're almost there." Barry's tone softened a bit.

He knew that without me, he would have never dared attempt a night like this alone. He also needed a second hand to carry all the stuff. One thing I was was loyal. A faithful companion. Like a dog. A really smart dog. That walked on two legs. When Barry went snake or turtle hunting, I was right there with him holding the snake bag or carrying the water bucket. When he was out collecting butterflies in the field during the daytime or collecting moths under the streetlamps in the center of town at night, I was his scout, calling to him whenever I found something special, or running to get his collection kit when he found something. When school was out and summer was on us hot and heavy, there was hardly a day Barry wasn't planning a bike trip to one pond or another, or to one of a half-dozen milkweed patches in town. And I was right there, always.

"Drew! Get over here!"

Barry had gone on ahead into the clearing. He stood by the two trees he had marked earlier that day that were just the right distance apart. He shoved the sheet into my hands.

"Stand on the bucket and hold the corner," he said.

I dropped the backpack and did as I was told. He pounded one of Dad's roofing nails through the sheet into the bark of the tree. Sap oozed from around the nail heads and stained the white fabric a rusty color.

"Now keep it straight and tight."

I knelt in the leaves while Barry hammered three more nails down the short side of the sheet. We stretched the sheet to the adjacent tree and repeated the process. We were both sweating when we were done.

"Looks like a pitchback for giants," I said, laughing.

Barry didn't laugh. He probably didn't even hear me, too busy adding the final touch: a wire strung across the top two nails. From the middle of the wire he hung the Coleman lantern, adjusting the height until it was dead center. Then he lit it up.

He stood back and admired his work. "There. Now we wait."

Lepidoptera. It was Barry's first love. Butterflies and moths. The butterflies were easy. The scent of lilac or honeysuckle attracted them like yard sales attract Sunday drivers. Tiger swallowtail, red admiral, spicebush, monarch—all floated in on the warm breeze to sip their last taste of nectar before Barry swooped his capture net and entombed them forever under glass.

The moths required a little more work; they came out after dark. But, oddly, they had a weakness for the light. Barry explained it to me this way. Most moths were nocturnal, choosing to spend their waking hours while their predators, the birds, slept. But because they navigated by the moon, the outdoor lights of homes, street lamps, even car headlights, confused them, drawing them out of the woods. On warm, thick nights, it was almost a guarantee the moths would gather wherever an artificial moon glowed.

And the closer to the woods the better.

In the woods was best.

"Throw me a Mountain Dew."

We sat on our buckets as the night seeped in around us and the cicada noise rose into the trees. In the campfire atmosphere Barry told me stories about Indian Rock, which was only a mile or so from where we sat.

"They say a whole tribe of Indians lived in the caves beneath the rock. And some are still living there to this day, but nobody knows they're there."

"Not-uh."

"Yeah-huh. I also read somewhere that when an Indian was accused of a crime, they made him

climb to the top of the rock during a lightning storm.
If he got zapped, that meant he was guilty."

"What did they do in the winter?"

"Well, nobody did anything bad in the winter
because they were too busy trying to stay warm,
stupid."

"Oh, yeah, right."

The second thing I was was gullible. If Barry
had said tomatoes were just big ticks filled with cow's
blood, I would have believed him. As my older
brother, he possessed knowledge and powers beyond
my understanding. For example, every now and then
as we sat in the woods waiting for our first catch,
there came a chalkboard-sounding screech high in the
trees. We also heard the occasional snap of something
moving through the underbrush just outside the
perimeter of our lantern. Each time, Barry waved the
flashlight like a magic wand, and shouted things like,
"Get lost you stupid animal!" or "Take a hike if you
know what's good for you!" I remember chuckling
nervously when the sounds appeared to obey Barry's
commands. There were times I wished he wasn't my
brother—especially when he teased me—but I had to
admit that night wasn't one of them. As the darkness
turned to pitch, it wasn't long before the first flutter
appeared against the clean white sheet.

They started off small.

"Wood Nymph ... Gypsy Moth ... Underwing..."

Barry called them out by name as he got up to
inspect each new visitor, his collection kit ready.

"Rosy Maple Moth ... Laurel Sphinx ... Tiger
Moth..."

As the night wore on, the visitors grew more
abundant, more diverse. The lantern not only
attracted moths, it drew big papery Dobson flies,
shiny black beetles, delicate lacewings, and praying
mantises. After a couple hours, both sides of the sheet
were dotted from corner to corner.

Barry behaved like a mad scientist, using
tweezers and cotton balls soaked in alcohol to subdue

his catches, laying the drugged specimens in the paper towel-lined cigar boxes we had brought along. As the time grew late, the moths grew progressively larger.

"Luna Moth—Nice."

"Big Poplar Sphinx ... Awesome."

"Cecropia! Holy crap!"

Barry had never caught a Cecropia Moth before. The rust- and cream-colored beauties with the six-inch wingspan were the centerpiece of any collection.

The first unknown showed up just after midnight.

It hit the sheet with a thud, showering beetles to the ground and causing the larger moths to take flight. It had landed on the side of the sheet facing the woods, so we couldn't see exactly what it was at first. All we saw was the shadow of something that looked to have wings but also appeared to have long thin arms. Barry and I watched as the squirrel-sized creature reached out to grab the fleeing moths, drawing them into what we could only assume was its mouth. The soft crunch of insect bodies was heard above the hiss of the lantern.

Barry grabbed his net and was about to give it a swoop when another, larger creature hit the sheet, which stopped Barry in his tracks. This creature appeared to have more legs than necessary. There came a gooseflesh-inducing squeal as the first creature fought for its life.

It had all happened so fast. I could tell Barry was afraid to look but more afraid not to in case he missed out on seeing something truly unique. That's when we heard the intermittent whoosh of what could only be described as gigantic wings beating in the night. The second creature, which we still couldn't see except for its shadow, dropped its prey and scrambled toward the corner of the sheet to take flight, but it was too slow. Something big then hit the sheet with such force it tore from the roofing nails and fell to the ground in a tangled heap. The lantern flew and landed at our feet. The thing inside the sheet flopped and rolled in the leaves as it tried to free itself. Barry picked up the lantern as we heard the chatter of its teeth, and the tearing of fabric. When a pretzel-stick-looking leg two inches thick poked out and a three-fingered claw gripped the dirt, my feet at last broke rank.

"C'mon, Barry, let's go!" I said, and took off for home. I had grabbed the flashlight and ran with it as fast as I could. It was a couple minutes before I realized Barry wasn't behind me, so I stopped.

I could still see the soft glow of the Coleman lantern in the distance where it lit up the woods.

"Barry?" I called.

A heavy-weighted stillness answered me. Then the lantern went out.

I stood frozen in the woods, the flashlight trembling in my hand.

"*Barry?*"

That's when I heard the beat of heavy wings high above the trees. A shadow passed in front of the moon. It looked to be carrying something beneath it. Then it was gone.

## 2.

Thirty years later, almost to the day, I pulled my car into my parents' driveway. I turned the ignition off and sat. It was half past eight in the evening. It had been a long drive from Ohio to Connecticut, but that wasn't the reason I was slow in getting out. I hadn't been home in over ten years, and even then it was just a one-night stay on my way back from a friend's wedding. As the sun rested in the trees and the day's warmth dropped into the mid-eighties, I stared at the house Barry and I grew up in. I noticed the once robin's egg blue clapboard siding had adopted a darker tinge, from mold more than likely. The old TV antenna on the roof had finally fallen over and now pointed toward the woods like a broken finger, still clinging to its rusted bracket. The dogwood tree near the front steps had climbed half a dozen feet above the gutters. The grass needed mowing but overall the yard appeared maintained.

Another reason for my hesitation was I hadn't told my parents I was coming.

I got out of the car and stretched; my spine popped in several places. As I walked up to the front steps and rang the doorbell, a sudden acidic wash coated my stomach. My father answered the door.

"Drew?"

"Hey, Dad."

We hugged. I'd always had a good relationship with my father. He was a big guy with a gentle demeanor. I've been told I'm a lot like him. The ten years had been kind to him. His hair was nearly all grey now and he had only added a few extra lines around the eyes. He looked over my shoulder toward the car. "Is Rachel with you?"

"She decided not to come," I lied.

When we stepped inside he shouted, "Jeannie! Look who's here!"

Again, not a whole lot had changed: I saw the same furniture, the same knick-knacks. The living room was clean and tidy but there was a haze about everything, a softness around the edges, and it wasn't dust. It was age. It was gravity slowly deforming what was once new into something old, flattening what was once round and rounding what was once flat. It was the slow steady crush of entropy.

It was also a bit warm inside the house. My parents didn't believe in air conditioning. A floor fan with an oscillating head stood in between the kitchen and the living room moving the warm air around.

"I think she's in the bathroom," my father said. "So what brings you home, son? Here, sit. You must be tired." He gestured toward the couch. "Want a beer?"

The excitement in his voice made me smile. It was as if I was the first sign of civilization he'd seen in years. "A beer would great right about now. Thanks." I sank into the couch.

"Your mother must have fallen in. Jeannie! We've got company! I'll be right back." He disappeared into the kitchen.

The television was tuned to a Red Sox game, the sound turned low. On the fireplace mantle sat a series of framed photographs. I got up to get a closer look. There was a photo of my parents on their wedding day. A picture of my mom holding Barry when he was a baby. Sepia toned pictures of my grandparents. A studio shot of Rachel and I and our daughter Shelly when Shelly was five. We were happy then, our smiles genuine. A school picture of Barry from second grade, his hair long, the look in his eye mischievous. There were more pictures of Barry: one of him posing in his Little League uniform; another of him in the midst of a field with his butterfly net; and still another of him on Christmas Day sitting by the tree with a large box containing a racing car set in his lap, a smile as bright as a string of lights. And there were more Barry mementos too. On the walls hung the best of his framed insect collections, the butterflies and moths artfully arranged by shape and color. If it weren't for my wife and daughter, I don't think I'd have had a place on the mantle.

"Jeannie, look what the cat dragged in."

I turned and there stood my mother. "Hi, Mom," I said. I walked over to her and gave her a hug, then kissed her on the cheek.

Unlike my father, the ten years had not been as kind to her. She looked much smaller than I remembered. Her greying hair had thinned and was almost brittle-looking. Her jowls had become more pronounced, the corners of her mouth drawn down into a permanent grimace, and the skin under her eyes looked yellow. But her eyes retained that flinty sharpness I remembered well.

"What are you doing here?" she said. "Why didn't you call?"

"It was kind of spur of the moment." I couldn't tell her I was on a mission to bring Barry back, because that sounded as crazy as how Barry disappeared in the first place.

"How long will you be staying?"

"Jeannie, stop grilling the boy." My father chuckled nervously. "He just got here. He's staying the night at least, right son?" He handed me a can of Narragansett.

I nodded.

My mother stared at me. She then let her eyes drift past me to the photos on the fireplace mantle. She took a deep breath. The air seemed to rattle out of her lungs. "I was just about to turn in," she said. "It's nice to see you, Drew. Goodnight." She turned toward the hallway. "If you get hungry, there's leftover chicken in the fridge," she said.

"Okay. Goodnight." I looked at my dad as I sat back down on the couch.

He shrugged and sat in the recliner. He took a deep swig from his beer and stared at the television. "Jesus H. Christ, will you look at that score." The Red Sox were down seven to nothing and it was only the second inning. He picked up the remote and clicked the television off. "Let's go out on the porch where it's cooler."

The sun had set and the sky had darkened to a purplish glow. The insect chirr had begun. There were two wicker rockers on the back porch, a small wrought iron table in between them. My dad and I settled in, the gentle creak of the rockers joining the chorus around us.

"Sometimes your mother and I come out here and look at the stars."

"Does she usually go to bed at this time?"

"Nope."

"I should have called."

"It's fine, son. Anytime you want to come home is fine. Our door is always open. Your mother will come around."

I'd heard that before. Always the optimist, my dad just took everything in stride. He respected everyone's wishes and never criticized anyone's ways. He was the ying to Mom's yang. It was probably what made their marriage work. Unlike mine. Once on the porch, Dad and I didn't talk much. He asked the basics—How's Rachel? How's Shelly? How's the job?—but beyond that we simply sat and drank our beers, stared out at the night and contemplated the mysteries of the universe. Or the mysteries of our own universes closer to home. Of course, I didn't tell him of the troubles Rachel and I were having. I'd save that for tomorrow. Right now I didn't want to spoil things.

Three beers and just as many shades of darkness later, my father rose from his chair. "Don't stay up too late," he said, resting a hand on my shoulder.

"I won't, Dad. And Dad?"

"Yeah?"

"Thanks." The thanks was for everything—for making me feel welcome, for making it easy, for not bringing up Barry even though my presence likely pushed Barry to the forefront of his thoughts.

"No problem, son. It's good to have you home. Goodnight."

"Goodnight," I said. I sat a while longer.

I stared at the woods, at the darkness beyond, and wondered if I would be able to find my way back.

Back when my brother disappeared, a search party was called in, but they were just wasting their time. I knew what had happened, but who would believe me? Maybe if I had said something then, something might have been done. But I just couldn't take the chance they would put me away in some institution. So I kept quiet.

There were two generally accepted theories as to what had happened to my brother. The first was that Barry got lost. Somehow he got turned around and walked deeper and deeper into the woods until some tragedy occurred—a fall, a broken leg or worse—and by the time the search party was organized his body had become food for the animals. The second theory was that he had planned the whole thing and ran away. Barry was considered a risk-taker, an adventurer, with an eye on bigger and better things. At thirteen, he was tall for his age and could very well pass for seventeen. In those days your identity wasn't as set in stone as it is now.

But I saw what I saw. As the years passed, I was able to put what had happened behind me. For the most part. I survived high school, and went away to college. I became a grade school science teacher. I eventually got married and settled in Ohio where my wife and I raised our daughter. But every now and then, when night fell and the moon shone like a beacon in the mid-summer sky, it all came crashing down.

So, this year, unlike previous years when the school break came and my home projects kept me busy throughout the summer (last year, it was a stone walkway; the year before that, a garden fence; and the year before that, turning Shelly's room into the study I had always wanted), I realized I couldn't put it off any longer. I had to go back. I had to know.

The look on Rachel's face when I told her I needed to get away was one of defeat. When I explained that I needed to go back home and pay some kind of long-overdue respects to my brother, and it was something I needed to do alone, she seemed to understand. If it helped remove the specter of grief that shadowed me from time to time, she was all for it. Besides, the break would probably do us some good. Our marriage had been eroding for years. When Shelly moved out and left us a couple again, her absence shined a glaring spotlight on how little Rachel and I communicated; and the saddest part was that neither of us seemed willing—or able—to overcome the deficit.

One thing Rachel didn't know was the research I'd been doing, piecing together all historical references to Indian Rock: the folklores, the myths, the belief systems of the Pequot Indians. I found references to the Thunderbird, a great winged creature that once flew the skies, but had been relegated to myth due to infrequent and unreliable sightings. My research also revealed that butterflies and moths were often used in Native American culture as symbols of metamorphosis: men dressed in winged costumes danced a hypnotic tarantella to the Gods of Sky and Thunder, while tribal members tranced on dried mushrooms laced with psilocybin ... Saturniidae—or giant silk moths—hatched in broods that appeared only once a year ... There were inscriptions on the side of Indian Rock that no scholar had yet to decipher ... People who lived near Indian Rock were said to have seen glittering blue lights in the woods and the sound of thunder even when the skies were clear...

All of this information was like a series of signposts pointing in the direction of my brother's disappearance. It was path I had to follow.

With my parents safely in bed, I headed out into the woods. It didn't take long to get my bearings. Of course, I brought everything I needed: a Coleman's lantern, a large white sheet, hammer, nails, and some wire. The same recipe that had claimed my brother.

It was odd, but as I threaded my way through the trees and undergrowth, the hot summer night pressing down like a weight upon my shoulders, it was as if it was 1983 all over again. Barry was yelling for me to hurry up, and I was rolling my eyes when he wasn't looking. It was as if I was guided by the memory of that fateful day. Though the woods had changed—the saplings that had once slapped at our faces were now as thick as my leg—the moon was still the same. Like a moth, I was guided by the lunar light. And it led me right to the clearing.

It was much smaller than I remembered, no larger than the area of a swimming pool, the two trees much fatter. I quickly went to work nailing the sheet in place and hung the lantern. When I was done it didn't look like a pitchback for giants, it looked more like a foolish man's poor attempt to rid himself of years of guilt.

I broke down and cried then, realizing just how much I missed my brother. And for the first time I began to doubt what I had seen that night with my ten-year-old eyes and my ten-year-old imagination. Maybe Barry did get lost and died somewhere out in these woods. Maybe I did cause his death by running away with the flashlight and leaving him in the dark. Or maybe he was living it up in some tiny South American village with a beautiful dark-haired wife and half a dozen tall, skinny children each named after a species of butterfly.

I must have cried for good long time because when I finally looked up, the moth sheet was covered. Insects both large and small; some with thin bodies and long antennae, others with fat bodies and short antennae, iridescent, phosphorescent, translucent, and just plain black and shiny. I wished Barry had been there to see it all. I know he would have been rushing around with his collection kit, muttering to himself in Latin.

I was about to call it a night when something hit the sheet so hard it produced a gash in the fabric. My heart all but stopped. My legs felt heavy as stone. I had difficulty breathing. The shadow of whatever it was scurried up to the corner of the sheet. It appeared to be chasing a large beetle. It caught it just as the beetle prepared to take flight, a miniature hand closing down on the bug and cracking its shell with an audible crunch. The creature draped several segmented legs over the top of the sheet to secure itself while it ate.

*None of this could be real,* I thought. I felt like I was suddenly ten again and Barry was about to reach for his net. Only this time, I didn't run. When I heard the beat of heavy wings, I stood my ground.

This time the sheet held. The creature slammed into the wire support instead, flipping over and hitting the ground with a pained squeal, its wings and legs momentarily knotted. It landed no more than six feet away from me. And it was big. The meal it was after flew back into the dark of the woods. My heart thumped as the creature on the ground righted itself. It straightened its wings with an angry flap. It then shook its head, and stopped; its angular face turned in my direction. Two iridescent, golf ball-sized eyes stared at me, seizing me with their gaze.

For a moment, time ceased to exist. Then the creature stood upright. In the glow of the lantern, I realized it was taller than I. Its shadow loomed even larger against the surrounding trees. Its mouth began to chitter. Its smaller forelegs, which were folded in upon its chest, extended outward. Its forepaws were not spurred; they were smooth and curved like grappling hooks.

All I could think of was how Barry must have felt that night, coming face to face with such an amazing creature, wanting to know what it was and where it had come from.

As the creature prepared to strike, I slowly turned my back to it ... and let it take me.

### 3.

My feet brushed the treetops as the creature carried me through the night. The downdraft of its wings was like a dragon's breath upon my head. The pain in my shoulders was excruciating. Its forepaws had pierced my flesh and were locked around my collarbones. I could barely stay conscious. But I had to see what my brother had seen.

We didn't travel far. In the moonlight, amid the undulating landscape of trees below, I saw a clearing. A dark shape occupied its center. I recognized it as Indian Rock. We began to circle, spiraling faster and faster. It felt as if we were falling. The night crackled around us. Blue veins danced in the air and Indian Rock turned into a great black pool. I heard the creature shriek as it dove headlong. Or it could have been the sound of terror being ripped from my lungs. Either way, I thought I was about to die. But I must have passed out instead, because I woke up some time later chilled and feverish.

I lay on a bed of straw in what appeared to be a small cave. The cave was empty. The surface of its walls appeared hollowed out as if by a thousand tiny chisels. Carved into the ceiling above was a large design that looked like two folded wings. As I stared at the intricacy of its pattern, it shifted slightly, a subtle movement that suddenly set my adrenalin pumping.

*It's here,* I thought. *It's right above me.*

Morning light shone just beyond the cave's entrance. I needed to move. I needed to get away and find my way back home. I got to my knees.

My collarbones burned. The puncture wounds were packed with mud. But there appeared to be no permanent damage as everything still worked.

As quietly as I could—although I believed every bend of my joints and beat of my heart was heard for miles around—I crawled to the cave entrance ... and was met by an immediate vertigo. I gripped the stone beneath my fingers as my sanity threatened to desert me.

The world fell away as I gazed down into the mouth of a steep chasm. A river cut a thin blue line perhaps a thousand feet below. Across this amazing chasm, in the near-perpendicular surface of the opposing wall, were dozens of caves similar to the one I was in.

*But how could this be?*

If it weren't for the pain in my shoulders, I would have believed this to be a very vivid dream.

But the memory of what had happened suddenly
flooded back ... along with a near-paralyzing fear that
the creature that had taken me would soon awaken,
and would not be pleased that its catch had scurried
away. I had been taken for food—or worse—I was
sure of it. And if that were true, I had to assume my
brother had met a similar fate all those years ago. I
summoned every shred of courage I had left and
chanced another glimpse over the edge of the cave
entrance.

In my favor, a network of leafy vines wove
their thick tendrils up and down the vast expanse of
the chasm wall. The full scope of what I was dealing
with didn't exactly hit me then. If it had, I might
have curled into a ball, unable to move.

*How was I to escape, let alone find my way back
home?*

But then the thought occurred: *There had to
have been others like me, taken, assumed dead by their
captors, and yet fit enough to escape; and of those who
had, perhaps a lucky few had survived.* It was my only
hope, and I clung to it as I slid my legs over the
stone lip, latching on to the thick vines. I began my
descent.

As kids, Barry and I would climb the two large
maple trees in our back yard and stand in the top-
most ring of branches just to feel the sway of the
wind. The climb up was always much easier than the
climb down, the correct route lost beneath my feet. It
was too easy to miss a branch or strand myself and
have to retrace my steps. Thankfully, the vines on the
chasm wall, some as thick around as sewer pipes,
were anchored firmly into the crevices by an army of
arterial roots. To add to the treachery, the large
leaves oozed a sticky substance when broken, so I had
to take care as my feet searched blindly for toeholds.
I had managed to descend the distance of a football
field before debris began falling past me. There were
movements in the leaves above. I couldn't be sure if it
was my captor or another of those winged creatures,

awakened by my passage, but it was crawling head-first atop the vines toward me, and moving with an agility I didn't possess.

By now, residents of the other caves I skirted were crawling forth into the morning light. One in particular took offense when my pursuer nearly crashed into him. A fight erupted, one protecting its territory, the other protecting its prey. As they squared off on the near-vertical surface, hacking at each other with their hooked forepaws, I continued my descent.

Halfway to the river the vines grew substantially thicker, the wide leaves knitted together to provide an awning under which I could hide. As relieved as I should have been, camouflaged by these pockets of verdancy, there were other creatures that occupied the nooks and crannies in the chasm wall. In these pockets the creatures were much smaller. I recognized them from their appearance at the moth sheet back home. They clung to the underside of the vines, huddled in the cool, moist shade of the vegetation. Their eyes popped open as I passed, glowing red like emergency exit signs. They made no move to attack me. Perhaps my size intimidated them. Or perhaps they knew the fate that awaited me, and were simply biding their time before collecting the leftovers of my skewered carcass.

By now, a dozen or more of the moth-like gargantuans had taken flight and circled the air between the chasm walls. As I hurried through breaks in the leaves, they began taking turns, swooping down in anticipation of when I was unprotected. The first one nearly knocked me from my perch, its forepaws barely missing my shoulder, splashing me with crushed leafy matter instead. Another quickly followed as I hurried for the next hiding spot. It was a sport for them. I was the poor wildebeest pup besieged by a pack of playful hyenas. One by one they swooped after me. I was still a hundred feet up from the river when I climbed out into the open, turned, and was startled by one of the creatures sitting perched on the canopy of leaves behind me. It reared up to lunge and my body reacted: I jerked backwards, losing my grip, and fell into the open air.

I must have tumbled several times over, the slap of leaves and vines teasing me on the way down, before entering the icy cold of the river below. The water encased me as I shot to the bottom, my feet burying into the sandy riverbed. When I realized I had survived, I opened my eyes.

The water was clear. So clear, in fact, I could see the sparkle of schist and quartz deposits reflecting like sequins on the sandy bottom.

I also saw bones; clean, white, long since stripped of their flesh.

And skulls. Some crowning through the sand as if the river was about to give birth; others buried to their eye sockets, staring at the sky as if forever cursed.

And not all the skulls were human.

That's when the current began to pull me downstream.

*What was this place?* the science teacher in me asked as I kicked toward the surface. *Was Indian Rock some mystical portal leading to the center of the Earth? Or was this some place altogether different?*

I didn't have time to consider the implications of my theories, because just as I was about to surface I saw shadows crisscross over me. I stayed submerged, watching the sky, letting the current take me further away, until the air burned in my lungs. At last, I surfaced, gasping. To my surprise, the moth creatures had remained close to their dens, circling in the sky like giant kites. None followed in pursuit.

I floated on my back, thankful to be alive. The cold water invigorated me. I watched the chasm pull away. The steep stone cliffs softened, opening into a wide canyon. Lush green vegetation replaced naked stone. After several minutes of floating lazily, I looked to the riverbanks with an eye toward swimming ashore.

But the riverbanks were also pulling away, the river widening. The current, which had slowed, had begun to pick up again. I now felt a definite pull to one side. I turned to face where I was going, kicking to try and slow my movement. To my surprise, instead of a continuous stream of water cutting through the landscape ahead, the river ended abruptly. Directly ahead was a ring of stone as high as the riverbanks. The river simply dead-ended, circling around and around. *It had to go somewhere,* I thought. My heart panicked with the sudden realization that the only place it could go was down. The darkness in the water ahead was not a simple cloud stirred by the rotation of the water, but the dark, glassy eye of a whirlpool.

I tried to kick free of the current, perhaps slingshot toward the nearest bank, but I was already caught in the whirlpool's rotation. The swiftness of the current increased as I neared the dead-end. I rode the surface of the water as it slanted downward, constricting and spinning in an ever-deepening throat. The sound of a million gallons of water flushed down a great drain now filled the air. Before it swallowed me, I prayed that the air I sucked into my lungs would not be my last.

It didn't so much feel like I was in the belly of a beast as I was being passed through its intestines. My body rode a smooth, dark tunnel, twisting and turning like an amusement ride, until eventually I was shat out into the calm of a deep sunlit pool.

Water had entered my lungs and I fought for the surface. The weight in my chest was so intense it felt as if I would be crushed. I swam toward shallower water, coughing and gasping for air. I heard voices—shouts of alarm—and footsteps running in my direction; splashes of water. Hands grabbed me and dragged me to shore. I was rolled onto my back. Hands cupped my head and air was blown into my open mouth. After an eternity it seemed, water gushed from my throat and the weight in my chest eased. I could breathe again.

I opened my eyes, my vision blurred by water droplets. Several men and women dressed in primitive clothing hovered over me. The man kneeling by my side—the one who had breathed life back into me—looked a lot like my brother Barry would have looked if he had only aged five years instead of thirty.

"Barry? I said, hopeful and yet bewildered.

He then spoke. "Drew?"

His voice was deeper but I knew then it was definitely Barry.

I didn't even have the strength to put my thoughts into words, because I passed out then from exhaustion and relief.

### 4.

I awoke some time later to the crackle of a fire and the soft murmur of conversation. I felt wrapped in a cocoon of comfort and feared that if I opened my eyes it would all be a dream.

"*Is he okay...?*"

"*I can't believe he survived...*"

"*We survived...*"

"*But he is so old...*"

"*Shhhh ... he's fine ... let him rest...*"

I lay listening to the words, my thoughts spinning, circling like a great whirlpool, always coming back to the same realization: I had found my brother.

*But what now?*

I almost wanted to continue pretending to be asleep so I wouldn't have to face the answer to this uncertainty. But I had so many questions.

When I opened my eyes, it was nighttime. A fire, built from several logs stacked teepee-style, burned at the center of a circular pit some fifteen feet away. A dozen or so men and woman, ranging in age from adolescence to middle age, sat on straw mats watching the flames. From where I lay, in the hollow of a stone boulder, their faces were indistinguishable from each other. The warmth from the fire radiated from the stone, keeping me warm. My wet clothes were laid out on flat stones nearby. I was naked but for a loincloth made of some tightly woven fabric cinched around my waist.

My waking must have spread quickly through the circle because the man sitting nearest got up and approached. He brought me a bowl of soup.

"How are you feeling, Drew?"

I sat up. I took the bowl Barry handed me, unable to pull my stare away from his face. "Is it really you?" I said. "But I don't understand."

"Neither do I. But here we are."

He sat down beside me. I was old enough to be his father, but the look in his eyes still recalled a time when I bowed to his every command. I instantly felt myself waiting on him to tell me what to do, *wanting* him to tell me what to do. When he didn't, I filled the moment with small talk, and drank the soup, which was very good.

"There must be something different about the time here," I said.

"That's for sure."

Together we gazed around at our surroundings. Beyond the immediate hard-packed soil of the village, the night carved a black landscape of tree groves and distant mountains. The stars overhead were startlingly bright and decorated the sky from corner to corner.

"I set up a moth sheet ... just like we did that night," I confessed. "Same spot. All these years of running, it was finally time for me to stop." I reflected on my actions. "I wanted one of those things to come. I wanted it to take me."

Barry stared at me. "Well, you're here now. That's all that matters."

I laughed and felt tears rush to the corners of my eyes. I hugged him, and I felt him hug me in return.

"Come," he said, "sit with us. Tell them your story."

I did. I told them my story. And one by one they told me theirs.

Mark, the youngest, looked a lot like one of my students. He had been riding his dirt bike across an open field when he disappeared. He was twelve years old at the time.

Shari, a woman in her mid-twenties, was beaten by her boyfriend and left for dead in the woods. She remembered the sound of heavy wings before she blacked out.

The oldest member, Charlie, who wore a thick, walrus-like moustache and long, greying hair tied back in a ponytail, said he disappeared in 1954 after a night of drinking. He had stopped along the roadside to relieve himself and the next thing he knew he was falling into a dream world. That was over fifty years ago. He looked no older than I.

The stories were the same, a different year, a different location, a different circumstance, but all had disappeared within a ten-mile radius of the Indian Rock, and all at virtually the same time of year.

"So how do I get back?" I asked.

My question was met with laughter.

"You don't," said Charlie.

My silence was met with more laughter.

"Believe me, I know what you're going through, friend," Charlie said. "I nearly went nuts my first week here. I wanted out. But once I realized this was my life—that the dream was real—I wondered why I ever wanted to leave in the first place. And you will, too."

Most of the people around the circle nodded their heads in agreement. A beautiful dark-haired woman, who hadn't told her story yet, wasn't nodding.

"How about you?" I said, directing my question to her. "What's your story?"

She stared at me. Her eyes were deep, wide pools. She appeared uncomfortable.

"Anja doesn't speak," said Barry. "She was born here."

"Born here? Where are her parents?"

"They're no longer with us," said Barry. "The Commons has existed for centuries, if not millennia."

"Commons?"

"Yes, it's the name that's been handed down. The word probably once meant something else, but over the years it has evolved to describe the feeling of this place. There is a balance here. A connection between all things. There is a peace and tranquility that cannot be found back in the old world."

"A peace and tranquility? What about those creatures that live in the caves upstream? The ones who wanted to eat me for breakfast?"

"The Konrak are the gods of this place," said Charlie. "They are the guardians that keep the worlds apart."

"Guardians? They entered our world and took each and every one of us." I looked around the circle for support, but no one blinked.

"The reasons for their actions are not completely understood," said Barry.

"They're gods," said Charlie. "They don't need any reasons."

I thought about that night Barry disappeared. Smaller creatures showed up first, like the ones I saw living beneath the vines. Maybe the Konrak were just keeping the peace, chasing violators back into their world. Maybe the people they took were just innocent bystanders, taken to preserve the secret of the Konrak's existence.

Whatever the reasons, I wanted to go home and Barry was coming back with me.

"There has to be a way to get back," I said. "They do it."

"But that would be sacrilege," said a mousy-looking women whose name was Mary. She had been abducted from her own back yard.

I threw up my hands. "Look, I don't want to stay here. I want to go home. Don't you understand? This is crazy."

"Is your brother crazy for wanting to remain here?" said Charlie.

"But he's coming with me. Aren't you, Barry? We'll find our way back the same way we found our way here."

My brother's eyes were clear and unwavering. His face told me all I needed to know. "I have nothing back there, Drew," he said. "My life is here." He searched my face for understanding. "The Konrak are amazing creatures. I knew it the second I came face to face with one that night in the woods. I was a chosen one. We've all been chosen. And now you're a chosen one, too."

"What about Mom and Dad?" I said. "It broke their hearts when you disappeared. Mom still blames me. Nothing was the same afterward. They lost a son. I lost a brother."

"But you're here, now. We're together again."

I never could talk to my brother. We were always on different sides of the planet. I guess now was no different.

I realized I wasn't going to get the answers I sought. With so many eyes on me looking to see what I was going to do, I did what was expected of me. I quit asking questions and adopted the pretense of accepting my fate.

"I could use a drink," I said.

Laughter erupted.

*"Gopi ... gopi..."* the group chanted.

It sounded like they were saying "goat pee." In fact, there were no goats, or chickens for that matter. As near as I could tell it was a completely agrarian society. The only ones eating meat, it seemed, were the Konrak.

Shari and two others left and came back with gourd flasks and wooden cups. I took the first drink and winced. The gopi went down fast but lingered along the way. I then chugged the rest to more chants.

"What is it?" I asked Barry, enjoying my second cup.

"It's a rye whiskey mixed with fermented berries and some mint."

It was actually quite good.

After several rounds of gopi, Charlie began to sing. It started out sounding like an Irish bar song, but like a bagpipes finding its full potential, the notes became sustained, oscillating around a central trance-like melody. The people seated around the fire stomped their feet on the hard-packed earth, producing a syncopated beat. The young woman named Anja rose slowly, as if summoned by the song. She stomped her feet and rolled her hips. Her arms intertwined in the air like serpents. She stomped and whirled, then started the sequence of movements all over again.

I was mesmerized by the dance, but I was mostly mesmerized by Anja's beauty. The cloth tunic she wore hugged her body like a second skin. She was sensual. She was primal. I could do nothing but gaze at her, lost in the coal-dark chasms of her eyes. Everything around me began to echo.

"The nights are long, Drew. Sit back. Relax..." Barry's voice trailed off.

The gopi had produced its desired effect.

I remember only bits and pieces after that ... Anja drawing close, reaching out her hands to me ... The singing growing louder, lifting me off my feet ... Anja's sweet scent as I danced with her ... The world receding—worlds both real and imaginary—while the fire roared from gold to red, to a brilliant pale blue.

Hours later I found myself lying in Anja's arms. Whatever drug the gopi contained had worn off. Water lapped at our feet. We were on the shore of the pool into which the river flowed from the mountain above. The starlight illuminated her features. When she saw me gazing at her, she smiled. It was a perfect moment, one I could have never imagined in all my life, and here it was, occurring after not even a single day in this bizarre but beautiful world. I got the feeling that, in this world, magic like this happened more often than not.

"What is it like to live here all your life?" I asked her.

She was so beautiful it hurt to look at her for any period of time, but it was a type of hurt I could get used to. I reached over and pushed a strand of hair off her forehead. "You know, back home, a relationship like ours would be greeted with backhanded whispers and disapproving stares. 'How did an old guy like him get so lucky?' they would say."

The look on her face alternated between understanding and amused confusion. Then she spoke. "My mother was killed by a Konrak. No one saw it happen. One day she was just gone."

She said it so matter-of-factly that, for a moment, I'd forgotten that she wasn't supposed to be able to speak. Or did I just misunderstand what Barry had said?

"My father went to look for her. He kissed me on the forehead and said, 'I will see you again.' But he never came back."

"I'm sorry," I said. I was so surprised by both by her speech and by what she was telling me, I didn't know what else to say.

She sat up and stared at the waterfall that emptied into the pool. The pool shimmered beneath the starlit sky.

"I used to sit here and watch the water, waiting for it to bring my father back. The river gives us everything. It satisfies our thirst. It bathes us when we're unclean. It brings us the chosen ones. It brought us you."

I sat up next to her. The skin of our shoulders touched and I felt the warmth radiating from her body. I moved to break that contact. "I'm sorry, Anja, I am not a chosen one. I still want to leave."

"I know." She turned to me. "Take me with you."

I didn't know what to say. I had come for my brother, but now this woman wanted to leave with me instead. This beautiful young woman I was beginning to develop feelings for.

"There is a man who lives in a cave," she said. "I can bring you to him. He is very old. He will know how to leave here." She got to her feet.

"Now?" I said.

"Yes." She pulled me to my feet.

Barry was right: the night was long. And it was about to get longer.

### 5.

Anja and I returned to the village. The fire now burned a normal golden yellow. Most of the villagers had either returned to their hovels or lay where they had sat, passed out from the night's excesses. My brother was asleep next to the mousy Mary. I told Anja to wait for me by the edge of the village. I crouched beside my brother and gave him a gentle shake.

"Barry ... wake up..."

He opened his eyes. "Drew?"

"Can we talk? In private?"

He rubbed his face with his hands and shook the gopi's residual effects from his head. He then sat up, glanced around. "I would say it's pretty much just the two of us. What is it, Drew?"

"I'm leaving and I want you to come with me."

"Drew..." He shook his head as he spoke. "You're not going to find a better world than this. We have everything we need. We have food and water ... and drink. We have the company of each other—"

"The river provides—I know."

He stared at me. "You don't know the half of it. Come ... let me show you something."

He led me past the collection of earth and grass hovels to a plot of land that looked like a flower garden. Small shrubs grew around its border. As we neared I realized what I thought were individual plants were small columns made of stone.

"Our children," said Barry.

Each of the miniature cairns were unique in their own way. Some were made of flat stones stacked haphazardly like a pile of playing cards, others were created using rounded stones, smoothed by the river, no doubt. There was a grace and sadness to their stillness.

"A cemetery?"

"A cemetery of children ... infants fresh from the womb. We've tried for years, delivering in daylight and dark, in the sunny warmth and the coolness of shade ... even in the very water of the river itself ... but nothing works. They take their first breath and it's their last."

"I'm sorry."

As a science teacher I know full well that in the animal kingdom environment is closely connected to a species ability to reproduce. And who knows what the trip to this other world does to one's virility. Although, at least one sperm and one egg must have survived the trip many years ago. "What about Anja?"

"Yes. She was the last. She's very special, indeed. Perhaps she will provide the seeds for our future."

This was crazy, I thought. Not only did I want to exit my brother's vision of paradise, I was taking their future's only hope with me!

"Barry, please, come back with me. There is nothing for you here. We miss you. Mom misses you. I miss you."

He smiled. "I'm right here, Drew. We can build a future together ... here in the Commons." When he saw I was unmoved by his plea, he said, "But you do what you have to do." He stared once again at the tiny graves.

"Goodbye, Barry."

I hugged him but he gave no response. He merely stared at me. As I walked away he said, "You're not going to like what you find."

My clothes were now dry and I quickly changed, joining Anja on a well-worn path that led through shrubs and high grass toward a wooded area. We were on our way to speak with a man named Ghislain.

"He is the oldest of the old," said Anja. As we walked I tried to calculate just what that meant in the land of the Commons. If Barry had aged only five years in the thirty since his disappearance that meant the influence of time was one-sixth that of home. It would also mean that Anja, looking no older than a young twenty-something was indeed very old.

Once in the woods, the terrain sloped upward. Stone outcroppings dotted the night like large farm animals lost in the forest. Soon the outcroppings outnumbered the trees, and shortly thereafter there was nothing but stone, a maze of columns and partial walls that rose twenty feet into the night. I ran my hand along these walls and the stone surface crumbled beneath my fingertips. As we walked among the ruins, I saw the glimmer of eyes peering out from dark alcoves. I also heard whispers, as if spoken by voices in a language no longer used.

"The old man's cave is near," said Anja. "Do not be afraid. His face is difficult to look at."

Before I could wonder why she would say this —after all, how "difficult to look at" could his face be? —the surrounding night was eclipsed. It was so dark I could no longer see Anja beside me. She grabbed my hand to halt my progress. We stood for a moment before she spoke.

"Hello? I have brought a friend. Can we enter?"

A voice came from deeper inside the dark. "Anja ... Sweet as the summer sun, soft as the summer rain ... Come in, young one. Make yourself at home." It was an old man's voice.

The darkness of the dwelling was overwhelming. The enclosure's smell was a mixture of vegetable root and potting soil. I put my hands out but felt nothing but cool air. There was a rustle of movement directly ahead.

"Hello? My name is Drew—"

"And you would like to know if there is a way back?" A laugh, like mud expelled from a clogged drain.

"Yes," I said. "I would like to know." It was odd talking in the dark. I couldn't see this old man but I could feel his presence.

"And will sweet Anja be leaving us as well?"

"I—I don't know."

Another laugh, followed by a whisper of words in a language that sounded a lot like French.

A shift in the darkness. Movement to my right. The sounds of a cup and spoon clinking together. The scrape of something metallic. A flame. The sudden illumination momentarily ignited the room, revealing a makeshift stove and a teapot. The illumination was quickly blanketed when the teapot was returned to its place, but not before catching a glimpse of the old man's hands. They were covered in scales. Or was it just his skin? Dried and flaking to the point where it merely looked like scales? I couldn't be sure.

"Some tea?" the old man offered. "By the way, my name is Ghislain."

"No, thank you, Ghislain."

"Please, I insist."

His voice was close, his presence strong. But I felt that if I were to reach out, he would not be there.

He placed a cup in my hands. The scent of licorice filled my nostrils. "Where you will be going, you will need it," he said. His next movement came from the opposite direction. The acoustics of the dwelling created the illusion of his being in two places at once.

I brought the cup of tea to my lips. The warmth of the liquid was soothing.

"Is he aware of the risks?" Again, the old man spoke.

"I haven't told him," said Anja.

"What risks?" I asked. "I mean, besides the obvious ones."

Anja took a deep breath. "We know that time is different where you come from. It is said the Konrak are not the same when they come back from your world. They are changed. It is possible you will be changed if you should return."

I thought about that for a moment. *What was the worst that could happen?* I thought. *I'd be a fraction of a year older? Younger?* Being with Anja made me *feel* younger. The gopi earlier and the tea I was drinking now only helped to solidify that youthful feeling. The temptation to stay was becoming greater with every moment I spent in the Commons. It was a sweet yet horrifying seduction. I had to leave before I changed my mind, before my ability to choose was lost to me forever.

"I'm willing to take that chance," I said.

Ghislain laughed again. "The Konrak will stop you if you try to leave. They will kill you if they must."

"I understand. Now, please, where do I go?"

I heard a more confident tone in my voice. I felt like I could complete any task. I wondered just how much of it was the tea speaking.

"Listen carefully," the old man said. "At the bottom of the great mountain, where the two cliffs were once one, there is a pool of black water as smooth as polished stone. When the black turns to blue, the membrane between worlds is thin. You must enter then. Feet first, or else you will have a headache when you reach the other side."

Ghislain shuffled away. "Drink up. *Bonne chance.*"

"Thank you," said Anja.

"Yes, thank you," I said, finishing the tea.

As Anja and I made our way outside under the stars we heard singing, a throaty warble that reminded me of birdsong. In the dark, however, it was the most unsettling sound I had ever heard.

We hiked into the mountains above the village. Though my spirits were buoyed by the prospect of going home, my thoughts were on Barry. A part of me wished things could have been different, that we could have grown and matured together, swapped stories of college and married life. A part of me wished I hadn't run away that night. Perhaps together we would have been able to fight off the Konrak and none of this would be necessary. But, in life, we all make choices. Back then, Barry had made his choice to stand firm, while I chose to run. Though the years had separated us, not much had really changed.

From the ridge we were on, I could see the village below and its communal fire burning at its center. Anja's slender hand gripped my arm. "Your brother is very happy here."

"At least I know he's safe," I said.

We continued on along the ridge without looking back. I believed I was at last putting the past behind me. Little did I realize the past is always there, lurking in the shadows, waiting for the moment when we least expect it to come out and show itself.

I say this because there were several times I heard rustlings in the vegetation as we made our way deeper into the forest, movements that appeared to shadow our own. But the vegetation in the darkness was impenetrable. *Were there creatures in the night hunting us? Were we being followed?* Anja appeared unafraid of the night and its myriad sounds, so that put me somewhat at ease.

By the time we reached the mountainous portion of the river, the stars had faded. The smoky grey of dawn cast a shadowy pall over the surrounding landscape. Ahead, the liquid black of the river cut a path through the lush vegetation, dividing the great mountain in the distance in two. At our feet, the whirlpool churned and roared. Anja was captivated by the sight of it. She closed her eyes and laid her hands against her chest. Her lips moved silently, presumably thanking the river for all it had given them.

Perhaps I should have thanked the river myself for aiding in my escape from the Konrak and delivering me to the people of the Commons. But I was anxious to move on. Home was just a half-mile away and I could feel its pull like the whirlpool below us.

We kept to the river's edge. I had expected for us to have to fight our way through thick undergrowth, but it appeared our route had been traveled many times before. Flat stones showed through the trampled turf. I asked Anja about this and she shook her head.

"My parents never talked of the ones who came before us."

"Is it forbidden?"

"No," she said. "The past has no meaning." Her eyes were as innocent as a child's.

"Didn't you ever want to know who they were? How they lived? How they died? Aren't you the least bit curious?"

She shook her head. "No."

"But you're curious about the Konrak."

"Maybe I only said that to be here with you."

I grabbed her by the arms. "Listen to me, Anja. I have a life back where I come from. I have a family. They need me and I need them. Do you understand?"

Her dark eyes looked into mine. I felt naked in her gaze. I realized my rules didn't apply here. It was impossible to explain to Anja things like duty and obligation, structure and tradition. All that mattered here were the feelings between two people, and the feelings Anja and I shared for each other were too strong to deny. Just our touch fueled urges in me I fought to suppress.

"I understand," she said, and she walked on ahead.

It wasn't the first time I was confused by her actions.

### 6.

As the sky brightened and the chasm walls loomed above us my wariness increased. I needed to find the black pool Ghislain spoke of before the Konrak awakened. There were caves on both faces of the walls, so even if we skirted beneath the protection of the massive vines on one side, we were still vulnerable to being spotted from above by the Konrak across the river. Above all, we had to remain quiet.

*At the bottom of the mountain where the two cliffs were once one...*

That could mean many things, I thought. The bottom of the mountain could mean the river itself. The pool could be the result of an offshoot, a circular dead end, etched by years of erosion. Or it could be another whirlpool. I kept an eye on the water.

We passed the spot where, the day before, I had fallen into the river. Beneath our feet, thick roots crawled across the path and into the water where they branched into a myriad of siphon-like tendrils. Anja stared at the collection of bones and skulls buried in the riverbed. She couldn't take her eyes off of them.

So far there was no sign of the Konrak. Even the smaller creatures that lived in the dark spaces beneath the vines were hidden from sight. There was only the soft, soothing rush of the river, and the feeling that my return to this area had been much too easy. I believed that at any moment shrieks would fill the sky and an angry horde of the flying beasts would descend upon us.

But there was nothing. The morning was so serene it was surreal.

We left the silence of the caves behind us as we ventured further upstream. The river bent and the chasm walls converged, leaving only a semicircular tunnel through which the river flowed. Daylight shone at the other end of the tunnel.

Anja and I kept to the path, which became a raised ledge hugging the tunnel's curved wall. The tunnel's roof arched overhead, its surface chiseled smooth like the Konrak's cave, only there were no surprises clinging there. Soon, darkness gave way to light, and with an awe and apprehension reserved for only the most magnificent of nature's creations, we found ourselves at the base of what was once an active volcano.

The walls rose to a dizzying height, disappearing into the low clouds that capped the morning. The river cut across the volcano floor where, at the very center, it appeared to branch both left and right, while still continuing on to the opposite side. In all three directions, the river disappeared into the mouth of a cave cut into the near-vertical wall. The rock bed between the branches was stepped, carved out by hand, creating a series of plateaus like the seating levels of an outdoor amphitheater. In addition, there were over a dozen stone perches spaced at regular intervals jutting from the walls above. Directly ahead, in place of a perch, there was a lone cave ringed by a small balcony. Stone steps descended along the wall on either side of the balcony to the volcano floor. The soft, reverberant rush of the water surrounded us with an eerie calm.

I felt like Howard Carter must have felt when he uncovered King Tut's tomb, or Hiram Bingham when he first laid eyes on Machu Picchu. But the feeling of awe I experienced was tempered by an ominous emptiness, a feeling of abandonment so

profound I nearly sank to my knees. The civilization
that had once occupied this land must have been
superior, but like all great civilizations something had
doomed it to failure. A quick glance into the slow-
moving river confirmed this fact. Here, the riverbed
was littered with bones; a slaughterhouse quantity
that sent chills skittering up my spine. I couldn't help
but envision Anja and I as the last two survivors of
an apocalyptic holocaust, the seed couple assigned to
start civilization anew. It was a romantic notion, one
that was quickly dispelled when I heard the beat of
heavy wings. A Konrak circled in the sky above. It
didn't attack. Instead, it landed on one the stone
perches behind us, as if to guard against our escape. I
had expected Anja to be fearful, but she stared at the
beast with a simple curiosity.

More Konrak floated in from the canyon, one
by one landing on the stone perches.

By now Anja and I had reached the river's
nexus. It was at this point in time streams of
villagers began entering the volcano by way of the
four tunnels. The people took their seats on the stone
tiers. I recognized several faces: Charlie, the two
women who had brought the gopi for us to drink the
night before, Mary, Mark, and Shari. They sat on the
steps in silence as if waiting for the start of some
predetermined event. I searched for Barry but he was
not among them.

I hadn't noticed but to my amazement the river
directly ahead, as well as the two adjacent branches
flowed away from the nexus. The source of the four
channels emanated from the nexus itself, a meniscus-
shaped wellspring that, when standing near, was as
black as a moonless night.

"Welcome!"

The voice echoed across the open air. It was a
voice I recognized. I looked up toward the balcony to
see a misshapen figure standing on the stone dais
above the river. Though dressed in what looked like a

bizarre feathered cape, the man who had spoken was Ghislain.

"Welcome one and all to the third and final day of the Replenishing. Let us begin."

When Ghislain raised his arms, the cape spread and separated. I remembered the scales I thought I had seen back in the near total darkness of his stone dwelling. I realized now the scales were short feathers … feathers I now realized would one day evolve into the wings of the Konrak.

I felt duped. I looked to Anja but she sat down on the nearest step enthralled with the priestly Ghislain, who eyed me with a smugness only power could provide.

There was so much I wanted to say. Staring at the layer of bones centuries deep lying on the riverbed, I wanted to shout my indignation to all assembled—a rallying cry for all to rise up and take back their lives. But a rumble shook the ground that sat me down beside Anja. The water at the nexus began to roil and rise, the dark fluid bulging like an eye from its socket. A bluish hue spread across its surface. Above the tunnel Anja and I had entered the volcano, a Konrak left its perch, lifted into the air and circled the sky above. It climbed high into the clouds, momentarily lost from sight. A villager approached the nexus carrying a burlap sack. It was my brother Barry.

I didn't recognize him at first. My mind still wasn't used to the idea of him possessing the face of a nineteen-year-old. From the sack he retrieved one of the smaller creatures that made its home inside the vines. The creature squealed as Barry held it aloft for all to see. Ghislain nodded and Barry threw the creature into the pool, where it disappeared not with splash but with a crackle of electricity. At that very moment, the Konrak returned from the clouds directly overhead, its wings tucked, its body spiraling head first toward the nexus. It entered the pool with a loud thunder crack, and disappeared.

Barry sat down beside me. The sack squirmed at his feet.

"Still collecting, I see," I said. The tone of disapproval in my voice was harsher than I had anticipated.

"The gretch are native to this world," Barry explained. "They are the lifeline that help the Konrak find their way back to us. It is a small sacrifice."

"You mean, human sacrifice in the name of religion," I said.

"You misunderstand our purpose, Drew. The Konrak are the most learned creatures here, and the most benevolent. That knowledge and grace has been acquired over centuries of existence. You and I, and those, with the river's blessing, joining us today—the chosen ones—are mere infants. We have yet to rid ourselves of our uncivilized tendencies." He pointed to the river. "Those bones you see are a reminder of our troubled past. This place is a memorial to who we once were, and who we can still be if the wrong people are chosen."

"But that doesn't give you the right to steal us from our lives."

Another Konrak abandoned its perch and launched into the air; Barry stood, watching it climb. He fished into his sack and pulled forth another gretch. The rabbit-sized creature struggled, its eyes bulging. I guess the Konrak's benevolence only extended to more advanced species, I thought. Barry raised the squirming creature over the nexus, and into the pool it went. The Konrak came spiraling out of the sky. With a gust of wind and a tearing sound it also entered the pool. The aftershock of its exit shook the ground. There was no splash. In fact, in its ethereal bluish state I had to wonder if the water was even wet to the touch.

"How many trips are made?" I said. I felt sick to my stomach at the proceedings, which to me was no different than what the Europeans did when they brought slaves to the New World.

"As many as it takes," said Barry, as another Konrak lifted into the air. "We have three days each year to add to our number. This year, on the first day our efforts yielded nothing. On the second day our efforts yielded only you. Today we hope the river will be kind."

I turned to Anja, but I was still speaking to Barry. "Why did she lead me to believe I was leaving this place?" Anja's attention was on the Konrak as it soared out of sight.

"She wanted you to see us. She wanted you to see who we really are. Her intent was not to hurt you, Drew. In truth, you are the first Anja has taken an interest in. You should be honored."

Though she watched the sky, Anja heard everything that was said. She turned to me and smiled.

"Your parents? Are they alive?" I asked her, distrusting now of everything I had been led to believe.

She pointed to a Konrak sitting on one of the stone perches. "My mother," she informed me. Then she turned and pointed to Ghislain. "My father."

My heart sank.

Barry leaned in. "Anja is very special. She is the only one in centuries to survive past birth. It was even prophesized. 'And one will be born who will lead us out of the dark and into the light.' And you, my brother, if you stay patient, will command a very special place in that journey. Our journey. Out of the dark and into the light."

My brother's eyes were filled with a strange look, as if for the first time in his life he admired me. He got up then and reached into his bag, repeating the ritual.

Prophesies and sacrifice, good and evil, dark and light—it was all nonsense, primitive beliefs for the weak-minded and the easily manipulated. I taught high school science. I believed in the rigors of facts and analysis. I had friends and family, a job. I was a creature of structure and routine; without it, I felt lost.

Before I knew what I was doing, I knocked the burlap bag from Barry's hand. The bag opened and the gretch ran for their lives; there came a collective gasp from the nearby spectators as the gretch scattered in every direction. Barry hurried to gather the frightened creatures but I held him back.

"What do you think you're doing?" he said.

By now, the unexpected delay had caused a murmur to spread throughout the assembled crowd. All eyes shifted to Ghislain to see what should be done. Ghislain stood on the stone balcony and pointed with a feathery hand. "Stop him!" he called.

Several of the larger men got up from their seats and started to approach. Barry merely stared at me like the big brother he had always been, the condescension in his eyes all too familiar. "Drew," he said, "did you really think you could stop this?"

Growing up, Barry had always been older, bigger, and stronger, so our skirmishes never escalated beyond words. But now I was the older one, and my lack of fitness, for better or for worse, had given me a weight advantage.

I pushed Barry back, anger rising in my throat. "You're a selfish son-of-a-bitch, you know that! And a coward!" I said, for all to hear. Barry's face transformed from one of patient smugness to one of embarrassment, and, at last, anger.

The men who had gotten up to stop me were almost upon us. But Barry decided to take matters into his own hands. He took a swing at me, but I was ready. He missed badly and stumbled. I caught him and held him in a bear hug. "But you're my brother, and I still love you," I told him before I rushed toward the nexus and hurled us both into the blue surface of the pool.

An immediate silence enveloped my ears. Like a sudden change in altitude, my ears popped. The silence was replaced by a loud rush, and was augmented by intermittent thunder cracks. It felt like Barry and I were falling through the sky—a dark, thick sky stacked up like a column of air. I tried to hold onto Barry as we tumbled and turned, but the turbulence of our flight pulled us apart. I must have passed out momentarily because I awoke with a teeth-jarring thud. I rolled and fell again, only this time the fall wasn't far. The smell of wet earth invaded my nostrils.

Lightning flashed and thunder shook the sky. Barry lay on the ground several feet away. I crawled over to him, dragging his body into my arms. There was a deep gash in his forehead. He opened his eyes and stared at me. "Why?" he said. The horror and indignation in his gaze made me cringe. His eyes then rolled upward as if trying to see the wound he had suffered. His body heaved and I felt his last breath escape his lungs before he became still.

"Barry?" I shook him slightly as lightning flashed again and the sound of heavy wings filled the night.

Indian Rock loomed above us. Several Konrak sat perched on its rim. They made no move to attack. They simply stared, like a jury of otherworldly judges, their faces expressionless, their eyes unwavering.

A stinging rain began to fall and something moved in my arms. When I looked at Barry again his face had changed. His features had wrinkled and sagged to match the forty-four year old man he was. His body felt softer, its weight redistributing in my arms. Barry would have been a distinguished-looking middle-aged man, I thought. A professor of entomology perhaps. But as I admired the glimpse into my brother's future, his face continued to change. I watched with growing horror as the aging process continued. His skin grew suddenly thin and fragile. Raindrops became like miniature bombs exploding against his body, separating skin from the muscle beneath. The muscle then separated from bone, falling away in gelatinous chunks, exposing both skull and ribcage. And finally, bone turned to a milky mush. In a matter of moments, the rain had washed away my brother's body until I was left with nothing but his memory.

Again, I heard the beat of heavy of wings, only this time the Konrak were leaving.

"Wait! Come back!" I yelled to them as their voluminous shapes lifted into the night sky.

I scrambled to my feet, hurrying to find a way to scale the twenty-foot height of Indian Rock. I found toe-holds in the moss- and root-covered stone. Saplings grew in the cracks and pockets of the granite monolith, and I used these to pull myself up. Several times thunder tried to shake me free but I held tight. When at last I reached the top I expected to witness a black pool, a watery meniscus like the one in the world of the Commons, but as I cried out again for the Konrak to return my fists were met with solid stone. The rain and blue lights had ceased and I was left alone, stranded on this stony island in the woods, weeping uncontrollably for what might have been.

I sat on top of Indian Rock for what seemed like hours repeating the words, "I'm sorry ... I'm sorry..." over and over again until my lips tasted of salt tears and my voice was hoarse. I was sorry for running away and leaving Barry in the woods that night all those years ago. I was sorry for putting off the inevitable and waiting so long to try and find him again. I was sorry for my wife and daughter who had to endure all the years of my not being present one hundred percent because a part of me was always missing, always distant, taken with Barry that night he disappeared. I sat and waited for the lightning strike—for the confirmation of guilt, the punishment—praying the old Indian legend was true, but it never came. Somehow the lack of that punishment was much more painful than any supernatural decree.

As dawn began to push the night aside, and the full realization of what I had done was revealed in the light of day, I climbed down from Indian Rock and made my way home.

## 7.

I tried to be as quiet as possible as I slipped back into my parents' home. I didn't want to wake them and risk being seen in my muddied and disheveled state. I was halfway upstairs when my mother came out her bedroom and called to me.

"Drew?"

"Yeah, Mom?" I feared she might come to the bottom of the stairs and see me, but she stayed put.

"What are you doing up so early?"

"Sorry, Mom, I didn't mean to wake you."

"Me? I'm an early riser. Always have been. Your father's still asleep. I'll put the coffee on and start breakfast."

"Okay, Mom, sounds good. I'll be right down."

I heard the refrigerator open. The water faucet ran in the kitchen sink. I climbed the last three steps to the top of the stairs, my muscles aching. I was suddenly very tired. I stepped out of my dirty clothes and washed up as best I could in the small bathroom. There were scratches on my chest and back. The puncture wounds from the Konrak were all but healed. I stared at my reflection and saw a much older man staring back at me. I saw lines in my face and grey hairs that weren't there before. It could have been my imagination, or it could be that I just never noticed them.

I shaved and dressed and put on my best nothing's wrong face, and went downstairs into the smells of coffee and bacon. My father sat at the table reading the Sunday paper; his grey hair leaned in several different directions atop his head. My mother busied herself with filling plates with food and mugs with coffee. My father looked up.

"Did you sleep well?" His face didn't register alarm. The look in his soft grey eyes held nothing but a father asking his son a question.

I nodded my head. "Like a log."

My mother placed the breakfast on the table in front me. The eggs were soft in the middle and crispy around the edges; home fries with garlic and a touch of oregano; English muffin, buttered; a spoonful of strawberry jam on the side—everything I liked and remembered from when I was growing up. I grabbed my napkin and broke down into tears.

"What is it, Drew? What's the matter?" my mother asked.

It took me a minute to compose myself. When I did, I felt the need to confess. "Mom, I don't think I ever said this to you before, but I'm sorry about Barry. I'm sorry you had to live all these years without him. I'm sorry he's gone."

My mother stared at me. The hoods above her eyes appeared to recede slightly; the dark circles fading a shade or two. She smiled. It wasn't a smile of joy; it was more a smile of remembrance of a memory held dear unexpectedly surfacing. The smile was also a smile of relief. She nodded. "I know you are. But thank you for telling me that. You're all we have. We'd just like to see you more often ... that's all. Now eat your breakfast before it gets cold."

I ate. I even had seconds on the home fries and the coffee. I was starving.

Later that afternoon, I called Rachel to tell her I had made it to my parents' house safely, and in a few days I would be coming home. A five minute call turned into two hours of apologies and forgiveness and resolutions on how, from now on, things were going to be different. And even after those two hours, we still had a lot to talk about. Years of neglect doesn't fix itself overnight or with a simple phone call. It was going to take some time and a lot of hard work. But this was one home project I was looking forward to completing.

I spent the next four days with my parents, at times feeling like a kid again, other times just feeling old, like time was winning, pulling my mother and father toward some impending oblivion. An oblivion I would one day also face.

And everything would have been fine and the secret I held would have died where my brother died, out in the woods by Indian Rock, but on the fourth night of my stay, a visitor came to my window. I could not be sure of course because I was awakened from the middle of a dream, but in my half-asleep stupor I saw a shape with two red eyes hovering outside. I rushed to the window, now fully awake, but when I stuck my head out into the night I saw nothing unusual.

But what I heard was familiar. An eerie sound pierced the calm of the summer night: the soft yet powerful beat of heavy wings.

# Your Basic Plot

### by *Curtis James McConnell*

I woke up on the wrong side of the bed. Under's a side, isn't it?

I awoke with a jackhammer heart. It felt like a prisoner with its back braced against my sternum trying to kick its way out through the bars of my ribcage jail. My eyeballs felt like junior members of its gang sawing through the ceiling. In such a situation, any side of the bed is the wrong side.

It wasn't really a bed, though. It was a pool table. I actually was underneath it. The floor was dusty, smelly and sticky. So was the air.

I squinted. I sneezed and angered my entire howling body. My spine went off like a short string of firecrackers with the sneeze. I'm glad I didn't hit my head on the underside of the pool table. Slate and skull don't mix. Except my skull felt like it had already tried.

I looked around. It was a saloon. Or a cantina. Or a whatever the Turkish word for what this was is. That's when I realized I had no earthly idea where I was. Not even what country. My jackhammering heart flopped a couple of times up under my Adam's apple and I seriously began to panic. Where am I? Where was I last night? What did I do and where did I do it?

Then the panic stopped. Not a screeching halt, an abrupt stop.

What are you asking *me* for?

Stranger.

Who the hell are you?

The panic resumed. No zero to sixty, no acceleration, just sonic boom muzzle velocity. I didn't know who I was. Or am. *Who am I?*

I rolled to a side and scootched out from under the pool table. The beer signs were English and Spanish. More probably American and Mexican. Amerexican. I don't even know my *name* and I'm inventing new words.

"This can't be good," I confirmed aloud. I looked myself over in the dim mirror.

"Nope. Sorry, Officer, can't pick him out in a lineup of one."

I stumbled around and located the bathroom. I staggered in place, peeing standing up. Nine minutes later, I mercifully slowed to a trickle. I shook, dabbed, rezipped and washed. Then I swallowed my flopping heart several times to get it to shut up and let me think.

I still didn't know my name. I insightfully slapped my pockets. Then I confirmedly dug through all of them. No wallet, no money, no loose driver's license. Not even a comb. Even if I were some weirdo who put his name on his comb, or even monogrammed it, even had I been such a person, there was no comb to be found anyway.

I could hear my hyperventilation whistling in my nostrils. I began to weep wretched, scalding tears.

"*Help me,*" I screamed. The porcelain didn't actually echo, but it noticeably rang.

I tore from the restroom and looked in one of the bar mirrors again. I saw a crazy man. A scruffy, crazy, penitent man. I would do anything if someone would just tell me who I am.

But the only one to negotiate with was a crazy man.

Why was I in a bar? I don't drink. At least, I think I don't drink. I think I don't drink, therefore I am...?

Fucked.

I am truly, most woefully fucked.

Whoever I am.

But at least if I don't drink, I should get the hell out of this bar.

Assuming I'm not in hell.

I looked around.

No three-headed dogs. Must not be hell.

Well that's a relief. I've eliminated hell.

One possibility down, every place on Earth left to go.

Okay, let's go back to what we know. I don't drink; time to leave the bar.

Time to ... no watch, either. That's okay. I'm clothed, I'm apparently intelligent, I'm not visibly wounded and moving seems to actually lessen the pain, so—

I put myself in motion. The wooden door of the bar was wide open. The rusty screen door was latched.

I took the hook out of the eye, turned the spring into a scalded cat, and got the hell out of there.

The street was dirty. More accurately, it was dirt. Dun-colored, diesel-smelling dirt. Third World dirt.

Still, I could still be in America. Any decent-sized town in America had its Third World sections. I was really hoping I was in America, because they were getting increasingly picky about passports and such.

God, I didn't even know what *year* it was.

Not a problem. That we can find out. Just keep walking, find someone who speaks English, or America's close proximity to it, ask them what year it is without revealing that you're a crazy man, and take it step by step.

Hell, if I'm lucky, maybe they can tell me who I am.

No such luck.

"Excuse me," I said to a guy hosing down the alley behind his flower shop and watering the groups of flowers that had just been unloaded in big white buckets from a truck with Texas plates, "excuse me?"

He looked at me suspiciously, as if wishing the hose were a gun.

I walked up, tried to smile disarmingly, or dishosingly, or whatever. "You speak English?"

"The hell you think I speak?"

"Sorry. I just—I'm, uh, well I'm lost. Can you tell me where I am?"

"The alley between Avenue D and E."

"I'm even loster than that," I half explained, half apologized. "Where—"

He sighed in exasperation. "Tanglefoot, Texas, the United States of America, western hemisphere, the planet Earth, the Solar System. Okay?" he challenged.

"Yes, I *know* all that, but what *galaxy?*" I shot back from the gunsight of my chin. "I just—I'm really, really lost, here. I've been robbed, I don't have a wallet, my head hurts, and I'm not sure but I think I'm allergic to flowers."

"And this is the part in the joke where the big, burly trucker says, 'It's not your day, is it?' and unzips his fly. Police station's that big red thing on the other side of those grain silos. Git."

"Ya know, I don't think anyone's ever said git to me before."

He began sluicing petals off the cement decking.

"No, I'm serious, I've never been gitted before."

"First time for everything. Wanna try for seconds?" This was over his shoulder, so I was pretty safe.

"I thought florists were supposed to be nice."

He turned squarely to me. "I am nice. This is nice for me. If it warn't, you'd be squishing when you walk to the police station." He brandished the hose as if this were still a possibility.

"Well thanks. Thanks ever so much."

He snorted in disgust. "I work for a living." I didn't know if I had a comeback for that or not, but he kept on going in case I did. "Any other useful information you need or can I get back to it?"

I winced apologetically. "What year it is, maybe?"

He squirted a shot at my feet—I hopped. "Smartass," he scowled, and pointedly turned his back.

I had crossed the street and walked a half block toward the grain silos before I admitted, "I was serious."

Though I was glad not to be squishing while I walked to the police station, that was about the only blessing I could count. What if they asked *me* what year it was? I'd have no choice but to let crazy man come to my rescue, and he didn't know either.

They were bound to ask me who I was. And they were bound to shoot me when they didn't believe that I didn't know. That's what I'd do, if I were them. If I were they? It's they. They sounds dumb, and nobody every says it, but properly it's "if I were they."

Except I'm not they, I'm me, even if I don't know me's name. Maybe me was an English teacher, because they were the only ones to lament the long-dead proper they.

Believe me, I'd trade all my grammatical memories for a pair of *initials* at this point. I chuckled aloud without opening my lips. Wouldn't it be ironic if my name were Ed Alley? Or E. D. Flowers? Or Grammar T. Fuckhead, there's a good one.

I'd probably have to get to the police sooner or later, but I really didn't want to without a more believable name than those three. I don't know if I was a cop or not, but I do know that they hate being lied to most of all. Or think you're yanking 'em. But that's a form of lying. Either way, they don't like it.

If a cop thinks you're being honest, you'll at least get a smile. If they think you're lying you'll get a phonebook upside your head and another chance to straighten up and fly right.

Like slate, phonebooks and skulls don't mix. Especially mine, which, like I say, still felt like it had found that out the hard way.

So I hooked a left before I got to the grain silos and walked up Avenue D. I minded my own business when I repassed the alley and hoped Surley McGurley and his Magic Unstoppable Water Cannon did the same.

I saw D dead-ending on me a couple of blocks up, so I hooked another left on some numbered street. I was already lost, so it didn't matter if I kept track of my turns or not. I was trying to find my way out of here, not back here.

To my left was a large institutional cube, its gray, scowling facade defying the pink tint the dawn was bruising the air with.

The cube had a chain-link fence with a barbed wire tiara in front of it, and in front of the gate were a bunch of men who looked scruffier and occasionally crazier than I felt. They waited patiently in line.

Deciding that I had found my people if not my identity, I got in line too.

It felt pretty good. This wasn't so bad. At least I could pretend to have a purpose instead of pretending to have a clue. They were as likely here to ask my name as the police, but could be reasonably assumed to be more likely to take "I don't know" for an answer.

I could smell bacon cooking. Sure, okay, I'll be hungry. Easy enough task to remember how to do. Be hungry and stand in line, some things you never forget. I wouldn't know about riding a bicycle until I climbed on one, but I could remember these two.

No one really seemed inclined to talk. I could remember how not to talk, so there were three things. Hey, I'm pretty good at this not knowing what the hell's going on business.

I remembered a phrase, though not who said it or under what circumstances I'd heard it.

"He didn't know where he was or who shot John." I was pretty sure that meant the guy was really, really confused.

I couldn't think of a phrase to describe how confused I was. I mean, for all I knew, I could have *been* John. I was pretty sure I wasn't shot, but really, if I had been, I couldn't remember it. What if I'd been shot in the head and that's why I couldn't remember being shot?

I clamped my palm to the back of my neck. No sudden pain, no moistness or blood-matted hair.

So I probably wasn't John, but I still didn't know who shot him.

I stood pleasantly in line, smiling to myself. When you're no longer in a state of screeching panic and have stood your ground in the face of a surly florist with a water hose, the simplest things can take on a warm fuzzy glow. And there's bacon! Yup. Things are gonna be oooookay.

At precisely some early time, I'm guessing, a saddened and bedraggled guy with a clipboard came out of a porch, down six feet of steps, and opened the gate. He had a hand clicker and we each got a click. He nodded at some, spoke single words to others —"Mornin'," or their name—and managed to offer each a small bit of hope though he himself clearly had none.

"It's my first time," I said.

"Yes." He used the clipboard to wave those behind me through, still managing to click and talk to me.

"We don't take you if you're drunk." Click. Click.

"I don't drink."

"You clearly slept in those clothes." Click. Click click.

"Yes."

"And they clearly started out being yours." Click. Nod click. Smile click.

"Meaning?"

"Meaning you can afford them new. You have a job. A home." He stopped clicking and the line stopped. "Martha's Kitchen is a homeless shelter. For people in need."

Everybody was looking at me, waiting for an answer I didn't have.

I thought for a second. "I think I need some help," I said honestly. Ordinarily, since I wasn't pleading and didn't appear frantic or desperate, they ought not to have believed me. But since I said it so simply, he evaluated me.

He looked about to ask me something, then nodded and waved me through, clicking me simultaneously.

We filed up the six feet of steps into a narrow enclosed veranda with a card table desk and two more shaggy people behind it. A security guard in a crisp white shirt stood behind them. His arm patches and the stripes down his black pant legs were gold. I have no idea what the two shaggy men swaddled in plaid and disinterest were doing.

Martha's Kitchen was a four-story cube (though I'm guessing there were thousands of stories over the years) which looked and smelled like a county jail or a 1920s hospital. For some reason, the porch and interior veranda with the card table were on a six-foot platform on roughly the first-and-a-half floor, with the top half of the basement under the stairs. Above us were, I assumed, domiciliary floors.

We trooped down another set of interior stairs into a combination grade school lunch room and Salvation Army assembly hall. Apparently, the first round of breakfast went to the residents. Some were just leaving down a hall that ran past the kitchen. A couple of forlorn gents with hairnets and trembling hands were doing penance with a bus tub.

Bacon, eggs, coffee, some thin white bread that was either toast or just stale, some powdered orange drink and donuts. Food of the gods.

The guy next to me smeared butter, regular and peanut, on four donuts. A couple of other guys made themselves some cereal from clear Tupperware containers. When one was nearly empty, its customer said, "Okay, Steve?"

Steve was another security guard, reading a paper in one corner. He looked up, nodded, and took a sip of coffee as he went back to his paper.

Hmmm, the paper. I wondered if I was in it. Even if I were, Steve didn't look like he was inclined to apprehend me. I felt apprehensive anyway.

The cereal guy reached under a counter and dug out a clear bag the size of a pillowcase and refilled the Tupperware. He then resealed the bag with a casual fold and replaced it under the counter.

Instead of filling his bowl from the bag, which I would have been inclined to do, the guy used some from the Tupperware he'd just filled.

People were looking at me before returning their attention to what was in front of them. No one seemed to be wondering what my story was. I had the words, "I was wondering that myself," in the chamber ready to fire. Some seemed resentful, as if I were slumming. Some seemed condescending, confident that I would learn something in time. Most hunched with life-weary, habitual protectiveness over their breakfast and ignored me.

Some prayed before they ate. I didn't.

I didn't know what to say.

By the time I finished the first plate, my appetite kicked in.

"Uhhh, can we get seconds?"

Those around me kept eating. One guy was reading a book which he or someone had highlighted with several shades of marker and pen.

"Is it okay?" I directed at him. I thought he wasn't going to answer me. He kept reading. Then he put his thumb firmly at the end of a paragraph and looked up with patience. "Can I get some more? That food made me hungry."

He looked around. "Guess everyone's got theirs. Looks like some left. Put your plate in the tub and get a clean one."

"Should I ask Steve?" I hissed conspiratorially. "He looks busy, I don't want to interrupt."

Besides, if my picture was in Steve's paper, he might apprehend me out of resentment for interrupting his reading.

Besides that, if my story was in there, I wasn't really ready for any answers yet.

This time the reader guy's pinkie was the bookmark. He peered at me, but couldn't decide if I was joking or not.

"That isn't necessary." I didn't know if he meant asking Steve or my sarcasm were what wasn't necessary.

"I'll just put my plate in the tub and get a clean one," I said cheerily.

There was a bus tub on a cart by the door to the back hallway. A gallon tomato can had some flaccid suds in it with a spoon handle poking through. I put my knife and fork in it. I slid the plate under a blue plastic bowl so old it was transparent in spots.

There had been a couple dozen of us in line. Most were still here. Sitting alone at a table near the tub was a skinny black man with a skinny gray mustache and thick gray hair marcelled back to his collar. He was wearing a long-sleeve flannel shirt buttoned to his Adam's apple. He sat upright, his hands in his lap with fingers twined and thumbtips together.

I looked at the blue bowl. It had two flakes and some gray milk in it. "Is cereal all you're gonna have?" I asked sociably.

"That ain't mine," he snorted at the bus tub. "Ain't havin' nothing."

"Ooookay. Just not hungry today? I am. I'm starving." I don't know why I was proud of this.

"Discipline. Cain't live without discipline. Man is a prisoner of his animal appetites." He took his hands from under the table and laid his stiff palms on the table, gazing ahead. He looked oracular.

"I know I am," I assented.

"That's not good. God wants man to overcome his wants."

"I know. God keeps telling me that, but I just keep getting hungry. I'm naughty that way."

He whipped a glare at me, then slowly creaked his wizened head around to face forward again. "You keep on. You just keep right-on on." That's what he said. Two ons. "God's gonna reckon with man. The bill's gonna come due and how you gonna pay him you ain't right with God?"

"Discover card?" I offered.

"Go ahead on. Make your jokes and eat your food." He licked his skinny mustache, suckling it a bit.

"Thank you. I will."

"You think you know, but you don't know. And by the time you find out, it'll be too late to know. But that's okay. That's okay, man will get his bill and each man's gotta pay it. You think you know, but you don't."

I got right around in front of him and leaned partway across the table to get at eye level. He stared through me. I smiled at him. I hope my eyes gleamed. "Actually. To tell you the truth, I don't even think I know. As a matter of fact, I know I *don't* know."

Anger surged up the veins and tendons along the side of his neck and he blinked his head back as if I'd slapped him. Then he blinked himself calm again and looked at me. He sucked his lips back through his teeth. The motion gathered his mustache through as well.

"That's the wisest thing anyone's ever said to me," he said. "That's truth, pure truth. I been sitting here nigh on thirty year gone," he slapped the table, "thirty *year*, people thinking I'm crazier'n a shithouse rat, balls dangling in the mousetrap, and you come along and truthify me. That's right, that's pure D right. You don't know. Ain't nobody know, but here you are first one knows he don't know."

"So *now* will you eat something?"

He started to tear up. He shook his head firmly. "I cain't. I just cain't."

I went around to his right side. I put my left palm on his shoulder and took his wrist with my other hand. I gently said, "You got to, friend. A man's got to eat." I gently lifted him. "I know you haven't gone thirty years—thirty year—without eating. So come on, have something."

"Every time I fall, it's the devil offering me food. I sneaks and I hides it like a thief, and we're all criminals in the eyes of the all-seeing eye, but don't nobody *listen* to me, and then I gits so huuuunnnggy," he wailed.

"I'm not the devil," I said. I knew it would be a bad idea to truthify him with the fact that, for all I knew, I might very well be. "I'm a man who's got to eat. Just like you got to eat. Now come on, let's get you some food that you can eat right here in the open, in front of God and everybody, not like a thief or a criminal, okay?"

"For real and for true? It'll be okay?"

"It'll be okay to eat, yes. Of course it'll be okay."

"Bible say man can't live on bread alone. Thass got to be evil-devil stuff."

"Not on bread alone, no. But that means in addition to bread. You have to have your bread too."

He sucked in his astonishment, his eyes popping open.

"My *God,* man, I been *blind.* Thirty year gone, I been *reading* it wrong. Got to have the bread *too.*" He seized my hand in both of his and pumped it with undying gratitude. "Mister, you done brought me an *epiphany.* An epiphany, nothing less." He threw his hands high into the air, taking one of mine with them. *"Hallelujah!"* He flung my hand aside. He twirled. "Hallelujah praise God I am *hungry.* I am hungry and he feedeth me the truth." He slapped his chest with two quick raps and shot his arm straight out and up, pointing at the corner of the ceiling, with his eyes down and to the left in obedience.

"Thass right, thass right, *go* ahead on, go to glory, and hit it onnnne time for *me*."

He scampered up to the stack of plates, took one, and daintily built a hummingbird smorgasbord on it.

I looked around. Everyone was staring at me. Steve's coffee cup hung arrested midway to his lips pursed to blow on it. About the room, half-chewed food sat in chipmunk cheeks. The guy with the book had turned his head my way and was smiling. A couple of people were nodding.

I winced in embarrassment. "Any questions?"

Some more nods and smiles. Eating resumed. I still stood there, clean plate in hand, wondering for the umpteenth time that day what the hell had just happened.

The skinny black man, by now finished with his first plate in he probably didn't know how long, got up to get some more. I offered him my clean plate as he drew near, but just ended up tracking him with it as he cruised by. He put a little bit of everything on his soiled plate and sat down.

He shoved half a donut into his grinning maw and used a forkful of eggs to ramrod it home.

"You poor bastard," I thought. Eating like that, that much and that quickly, would make someone with regular eating habits sick. This furtive-feast and ostentatious-famine guy's malnourished guts were going to collapse in on him and then go nova.

We all gotta duck when the shit hits the fan. Plus, I didn't want to be around when he blamed me for it and got me thee behind him, Satan. I tucked his epiphanous gratitude into my back pocket to wipe his sweat off my palm, tucked my clean plate edge-up in the bus tub, and slid back up the stairs.

Whatever job they'd been doing as we came in, the two shaggy men and Steve's coworker were gone. The card-table desk had some flyers on it for various twelve-step programs. There were a couple of clipboards with some intake forms and chained pens. I thought about filling one out, but the first question was, of course:

Name_____.

The first sheet on the clipboard was technically a half-sheet cut horizontally and tilted vertically for its paragraphs and bullet-points of instructions about conduct I must be willing to exhibit in order to be accepted at Martha's Kitchen—basic honesty, cleanliness and good-faith type behavior I could readily comply with. I read it again. Yup. Can do. No problem. I flipped the half-sheet over the clipboard clip and looked again at that first blank imposing enough to keep Mongolian hordes out of the empire.

Name_____.

The half-page of cheat codes had informed me that I didn't have to give my full name, but encouraged me to provide something. I flipped back and confirmed this, then flipped again to the first full page. I couldn't even come up with a fake name, because what if it was really my real name? Putting my real name and thinking it was a fake name seemed somehow criminal to me, like deception squared or something.

I could neither come up with my real name, nor could I think of any name that would be distinguished from my real name, because I had no way of knowing what it was distinguished from.

"Well, that's horrifying," I sighed.

Feeling like a harmless, befuddled, pitiful old woman signing an Inquisition confession of witchcraft, I took a preparatory breath and carved a defiant X on the Great Wall.

"My God," I breathed, "that can't be right."

I thought about squeezing a Dr. in front of the X, or maybe even a Mr.

Feeling that being utterly adrift was bad enough without being pretentious about it, I moved on to the next question and didn't look back.

Since no one was around, I let the several pages of intake form interview me and sometimes spoke aloud as I answered. "No, I don't have tuberculosis. I *hope* I don't. Just put no."

Stuff like that.

It became increasingly apparent that "I don't know" wasn't an acceptable answer, and was rarely provided as an option for me to put a check by. Sometimes they offered me N/A, but my problem was N/A can actually stand for several things which were not always a distinction without a difference.

For instance—Family History questions. It may or may *not* have been *applicable,* the answer may or may *not* have been *available,* and I wasn't providing *no answer,* I just didn't know what *answer* I had *available* to *apply.*

Like tuberculosis, with some of them I hoped the answer was no, but the explanation for why I didn't know it was no was complicated (and unknown), so I just put no.

A haggard, middle-aged either doctor or nurse trudged by in squeaky, white orthopedic shoes. She had a stethoscope draped like an office party drunkard's tie around her thick, creased, bowed neck. She was hunched forward like she was pulling a plow. She was carrying a sphygmometer, and if you understand how I could know that word and not know my own name, you can gauge the levels of my frustration and panic.

"Hi, can you help me?"

She stopped near me but didn't exactly look at me. She waited like a plow mule for the reins' lash.

"I know people don't end up here unless they need help, but I really, really need some help. I know, I know, everybody's desperate when they first get here, but mine's a special case—"

"Everyone's is special," she sighed.

"Yes, of course they are, but mine's special-special. You see, I don't kn—could you at least look at me, it's kind of awkward talking to your ear."

She chuckled to herself and swung her ponderous bulldog head slowly to face me. "Isn't that what ears are for?"

"I don't know who I am," I confessed shamefully, but looking right into the pendulous jowls beneath the pendulous bags beneath her weary, gray-flecked eyes.

"You what?"

"I don't know—"

"—You're serious?"

"As a heart attack." I pointed to the blood pressure cuff.

If you've ever seen a plow mule turn into an ambulance, and we all have, you'll know how quickly she sat me down and strapped on the cuff. She even clamped her palm with maternal tenderness onto my non-fevered forehead.

"Give it to me straight, doc," I growled B-movie-aly. "How long have I got?"

With some embarrassment mixed with punitive withdrawal, she took her hand away and snarled, "Not long, if you slough me off like that. There is some concern here." She grunted as if to say "Oh for heaven's sake, what am I doing?" She didn't say it, she just packed the meaning of those words into an irritated grunt, removed the stethoscope disc from my arm and ripped open the Velcro cuff.

"You're not dizzy? 'Kay, come with me, let's get you someplace where I can examine you better. I was on my way there anyway."

"Just for fun, though," I muttered truculently.

"Huh?"

"Nothing. Just—I was just—you know how you could be wanting to go someplace and someone says, 'Hey, let's go to that place,' and all of a sudden it's like you *have* to go to that place, so you sigh and say,

'Okay, I was gonna go there anyway. Just for fun, though.' Ya know?"

She stared at me. I momentarily thought I'd forgotten I was Martian and didn't know how to speak English, or even Earthianese.

"You know?" I tried again.

"No. I don't even know how I would know something like that."

She reached her palm for my forehead again, then took it back. "I was going to see if you had a concussion, but now I just think you've taken a severe blow to the head."

"Isn't that what a concussion—?"

"Concussion's actual, I was talking metaphorical."

"Ahhhhhh, a metaphorrrrical severe blow to the head."

"Exactly."

"And what's a contusion? Is that a blow to the head too?"

She took my elbow and scooted me at a decidedly unplodding pace down the hall. "Just a hundred-dollar bruise on your chart."

I thought I might trip over my own still-startled feet. "So bruises are free?"

She stopped us. Using my elbow, she turned me to face her.

"Especially for you. Hear me?"

I looked. I nodded.

"Do you understand me?"

"Your words? Yes. Your meaning? Not so much."

"If you genuinely do not know who you are—and you've convinced me you don't, despite your flippancy—then this is serious. Something has happened to you. It happens all the time, except they're always faking it. But something has happened to you."

"Something serious," I said flatly.

Still holding my elbow, she steered me down the hall again, but at a less urgent pace. My feet thanked her and settled into her rhythm.

"By definition, something serious."

"I haven't stubbed my toe," I rephrased.

"At the very least, you have stubbed your brain, but even that's serious."

"Because it's my brain, I get it. I was afraid of that."

"Good, because you were acting like you didn't have sense enough to be afraid. We're gonna need full and complete co-operation on this one, full disclosure, got it?"

"You don't know how glad I am I found you. Because I've been really scared ever since I woke up."

"I can imagine."

"I mean really scared. Like panic at the most fundamental level scared."

"Mm-hm."

"So I'm really glad you came along."

"Message received, sir."

I stopped us. "I left my X back at the shaggy station," I said.

Both her eyebrows lifted. "Is this metaphorical or concussion?"

"Huh? Oh, uh, actual. I was filling out the intake form back at—"

She engaged the tractor beam on my elbow and we were in third gear down the hall as she said, "We'll get it later. Or get you another one."

"I think I should explain. I'm not crazy. When I came in for breakfast these two shaggy guys were sitting at tha—"

"Roger and Emmitt. Gotcha. We're on the same page now. I was thinking ex-wife, but you didn't know what to put for a name, so—"

"Oh *thank* you," I said. "I know it sounds crazy, if you don't have the codebook."

"Well fear not, my good man. Fortunately, I was a crypto-tech in the Navy."

"Think maybe I was too?"

By now, we were there, wherever there was. I was already seated, strapped this time into a tabletop sphygmometer, my eye pried open by the same claw that had pinched off the circulation in my elbow, and a bright gleaming light prying open the back of my eyeball.

"Couldn't say." I could see her lips square off in concentration, her jowls tighten.

"That's funny," I said humorlessly, "neither could I."

Looking North from the third floor of Schotte and Waite Hospital, Tanglefoot, Texas, is nothing but trees and the Kyle Hotel.

I have strong memories of innumerable events from throughout my life. I can neither place me fully in them, nor them fully in time. The names haven't been changed to protect the innocent, they've been redacted in the interest of rational security.

One such memory is of a friend of my uncle changing the starter in my car. It wasn't my first car, but it was one of them. It seems I gave several tow truck drivers from my teens an opportunity to remind me, "You should be dead," before plotting the twenty minutes it would take them to get the strap or the hook under a stable enough part of the car to get it out of whatever ditch I'd plowed it into. This time, the car was fine with the exception of the starter.

I can't recall the friend's name. But he was a taciturn, lanky Texan, with a farmer's patience and a postman's work ethic. He stood behind my uncle when introduced, nodded, took the new starter from me, and inched his ropey body under the car without jacking it up for elbow room.

It's rude to hand someone your problem and go sit inside and drink sweet tea and watch TV. My uncle and I stood near the front bumper the way a horse will come and simply stand near a horse felled by illness. You do nothing and say nothing, because there's nothing to do or say. Standing there is the least you can do, but it turns out the least you can do is all you can do.

We could hear various bumps of knuckles on casing, various grunts of bolts that won't unscrew and then do, various Excalibur clanks of wrenches ringing on concrete.

At one point, my uncle's friend said, "Hmmm, that's odd."

Since he didn't elaborate, and since it was my car and my fault he was here, I prompted, "What is?"

A few moments of breathing from beneath my small car and then, "There's a big dent in the casing on this starter."

My uncle and I mulled this for about fifteen seconds of silence when the friend commented, "And I'm beginning to see why."

Tanglefoot locals (of which I apparently am now one) refer to Schotte and Waite as Sit and Wait.

I'm beginning to see why.

It's been a month since I woke up in Mildred's Bar, which opens into an alley between Second and Main Streets. The back door leads to the back yard of a sagging house on Second. No one in either building remembers me being there that night. The owners of both disavow all knowledge of me, though to latch the screen door the last one there would have had to exit through the back door, lock it, cross the back yard to the house, unlock it, and make his getaway on Second without waking anyone in the household including the noisome dog chained to the only gate leading from the back yard.

Detective Dan Petrucha of the Tanglefoot PD says, "You might as well be in Camp X-Ray, hoss. I got a better chance of the dog ID-ing you. Whoever you are and whatever you were doing there, you did it after closing hours and off the radar."

Dr. Hannah Olverstedt, she of the elbow rudder technique, asked me many questions that day. I told my story many times over. To her, Officer Geoffrey

Fudge, Detective Dan, and a cast of thousands without screen credit. I was given field tests, clinic tests, diagnostic tests, X-rays of my brain, blood tests, everything but an MRI, which was deemed too expensive to order for someone without a name to give to the creditors when I couldn't pay.

At the end of that first day of the rest of my life, Dr. Olverstedt gave me a notebook and a small digital recorder. "Go over it again, every day. Anything comes up, any clue that'll help us out, write it down, or push record here. Write down everything."

As you may know, this is my eighth notebook. I've lost track of my visits to Sit and Wait. I sleep at Martha's Kitchen, I traipse over here sometimes twice and once three times in one day, and I tell my story. I've been on local news, a billboard, and Nancy Grace. Nobody's seen me, or if they have, for whatever reason they haven't fessed up.

About the third day, I was taken to a speech pathologist. He had me say words like water and telephone and Harvard and begin. He seemed fascinated that I said *eye-ther* instead of *ee-ther,* but other than that was dismayed that I spoke with no definite regional accent. No Cajun Patois. No Yankee Talk (talk was one of the words he had me say), no New York or Jersey or Philly ("There's a *difference?*" I asked, unanswered). I didn't have a midwestern, a southwestern or a southeastern accent or inflection. I wasn't from Georgia or Virginia ("There's a *difference?*") nor Wisconsin-Michigan, Nebraska, California, New Mexico or Southern Texas, Newfoundland, Quebec or the rest of Canada.

Wherever it was, I wasn't from around there, was I, boy?

My flat, bland, inflectionless baritone was dubbed by the speech pathologist to be "generic nationwide newscaster bland," trained not to offend by betraying I was from somewhere else. Which is odd, because both the little gal on the local TV station and the little jalapeño cutie on the Spanish radio station sound like Gomer Pyle when they read the news. They had me say words. They tested my motor skills and the nerves in my feet. A slight palsy in my right foot, so slight, they assured me, that I might never know I had it if a trained professional hadn't been intensely looking for it. "So get dressed and I'll meet you in the consulting room."

There are two chairs in the specialist's consulting room, facing the consultant's desk. I'd never sat in the second one. The first one had a rip in it, but I went and sat in it as unconsciously as I'd just tied my shoelaces, a memory that had survived my inexplicable memory wipe.

In fact, probably ninety-nine percent of my accessible memory survived the wipe. I remember everything after waking up under that pool table with, as one of the Sit and Wait specialists said, "astonishing accuracy." I remembered with less astonishing accuracy things from before I was four. Other things, I can remember them happening, but not when, particularly relative to the whens of other events. Dr. Specialist-face says that's actually normal, though my ability to pinpoint exact sequences in distant memories is more fragmented than most.

I can remember how to tie my shoes, but not if I learned to do that or to read first, for instance.

He said most amnesiacs—most meaning about eight of the eleven genuine cases ever—retain the deeper, more distant memories, as do most people. Skills ingrained for decades can't be erased by whatever blotted a section of my brain. Most facts and skills and memories are filed in several parts of the brain, connected to several others, and aren't lost so much as they're misplaced or have their retrieval mechanisms disrupted.

My case was particularly perplexing because, for instance, I could neither write my name nor say it. Some words that we can't recall and say can be recalled and written. By neither method could I retrieve the names of anyone from pre-event days. Not only could I not remember the name of my uncle's friend who'd changed my starter, I couldn't remember my uncle's name. That would normally convince them I was one of the fakers, but didn't, for reasons they couldn't name either.

One of the specialists tried to lead me to describe my condition by saying, "Is it that your name is on the tip of your tongue but you just can't say it?"

"I don't think so. I know that feeling, like it's somewhere and I just have to find it. Like I'd know it if I heard it. But that's not what my brain does when I go looking for my name. It's not a sealed envelope, the envelope just isn't there."

He literally scratched his head.

Trees and the Kyle Hotel. Schotte and Waite was built on the tallest hill in Tanglefoot, what was then its southernmost point. Even then, the houses were hidden by trees. It's really quite pleasant. The view from the third floor is quite pleasant as well. My problem is, I'm a guy with no memory and apparently they expect me to memorize the north view, down to the last pecan on the northernmost tree. They certainly make me sit and wait here long enough to do so. For a guy with no memory, that's a particularly vexing task.

So I sit here, and I write. I'm a local celebrity whom nobody cares about, whose story is boring to everyone but they ask it anyway. So I've written it again, and gone through it again, and joined all investigative personnel concerned in shaking my head at it, again.

A few days into my new life, Officer Fudge came and picked me up and drove me over to the county seat. There, a deputy digitized my prints.

We got the results yesterday. Detective Pitrucha brought them to my bedroom.

I'm not a criminal, or if I am I'm an exceptional one who's never been caught. I'm not a veteran (or AWOL), an employee in one of the more progressive school districts, a banker, I'm not connected in anyway with law enforcement, or a government contractor. I'm not a doctor or a lawyer.

"What about Indian Chief?"

Detective Dan doesn't get my jokes. Which hardly seems fair, I get his.

"You're also not from Tanglefoot," he answered.

"And we know this how?"

"Officer Fudge doesn't know you. Fudge knows everybody."

"Maybe *I'm* Officer Fudge and he stole my identity."

"He'd know that too," Detective Dan said. "He'd know who you were before he stole it."

"That doesn't make sense."

Detective Dan shrugged. "Few things do."

I said, "Well, you got me there."

"Cheer up, guy. I'm still working on my Man from Mars theory."

"What about Camp X-Ray?"

"That's it, buddy. You've solved it. You're an international terrorist, you—"

"Suspected terrorist," I emphasized.

Pitrucha tossed me a bone of a chuckle and continued. "And you broke out of a secret government institution, swam ninety miles to Florida, then across the Gulf of Mexico to Galveston, hitchhiked to Tanglefoot and went to sleep under a pool table in a Mexican beer joint."

"It's all coming back to me."

"Case closed." Detective Pitrucha dusted his hands.

"Now let's work on world hunger."

"I'll settle for our hunger. Wanna go someplace besides the cafeteria? My treat."

I grumped, "It'll have to be."

"Don't people send you money?"

"Checks all the time. I tried to cash one, open an account. She actually asked me, in all seriousness, if I had an ID."

He chuckled as I straightened my bed in compliance with my half-sheet of certain behaviors I had agreed to comply with.

"Oh, and this was beautiful. One of those times when God must love you, because the timing was the kind of timing you could never put in a movie, because the audience would call bullshit. I actually looked up at the plasma TV and said, 'Well, that's me talking to Nancy Grace.'"

"That is beautiful," he concurred.

"Didn't do any good, because then she said to open an account, they had to give the Feds my Social Security number."

"Uh oh." Then he ambushed me. "What's your social, sir?"

I stopped. "The old cloaked in the commonplace trick. Nice try."

"You looked like you were about to say something. Even a first number would help."

"Except I wasn't. That is, I started to, but then I realized I had no starting number."

He shook his head, giving up. "You just better hope I find out you were holding out on me all along."

"You ever take Algebra?" I asked as we got my jacket.

"Three years. Half a cred in Trig, dropped out first week of Calculus."

"And now it's time for another thrilling adventure of Trig Calculus, Boy Detective."

"And you've taken *how* many hits of acid today?"

"Just the four. But they were purple."

"So *anyway*."

"Yeah, yeah. I was just asking because it's like solving for *x*, ya know? I keep thinking this is all just some really big word problem, and all I gotta do is take it one phrase at a time and solve for *x*."

That was yesterday. Sitting here, waiting to have the results of yet another test explained to me (usually the explanation is they can't explain it) and looking North at trees and the Kyle Hotel, I'm about ready to seriously entertain Detective Dan Pitrucha's theory and demand diplomatic immunity at the Mars Embassy. I'm also tired of writing. Maybe I'll read for a while.

Yesterday, *she* asked for me at the shaggy station at Martha's Kitchen. Either Shaggy Roger or Shaggy Emmitt came and told me. We're not allowed guests in the domiciliary. I was gonna have to put on my shoes and go meet her in the cafeteria.

"I'm busy writing in my notebook," I tried. "Dr. Olverstedt—"

"You don't even have it out," Shaggy One or Two pointed out.

I tried another one. "I was about to be busy writing in it."

"Ooookayyyy," he taunted. "If that's the way you want it." He turned with exaggerated carelessness to go.

"Is she *that* good?"

"Better."

"Better as in better looking, or better as in I better prepare myself because she knows who I am?"

He gave a considered answer. "As in better hope if she knows you, she's not related to you in any way, unless you're from Arkansas."

"That good, huh?"

"Three minutes, or I'm making a move myself."

I was pretty sure the shaggies were gay. I bent for my shoes.

"Very funny," I yelled from the cafeteria doorway back up the stairs.

"She went to the bathroom," a shaggy scolded as I'd taken three steps going back up.

"Oh. I knew that."

We all have our comfort zones. Mine was the chair I usually tried to sit in while I ate. It was the one I'd used that first day. I hadn't planned on sitting there. I thought about the ripped chair in the consulting room. I looked down. My shoelaces were tied. I reminded myself that this was the type of automatic activity that most people's memories don't bother to log.

Still, it bugged me a little that my memory hadn't logged it. Anyone who has ever known panic as deep as I felt the first time I was unable to access critical data will understand how close I get to panic every time I notice I haven't logged inconsequential data. My brain can remind me that it is in my evolutionary interest not to log tons of such irrelevancies, but my memory also remembers the time it couldn't remember and inches toward the panic button.

Metaphorical, not concussion.

The concussion came when she slinked scintillatingly into the cafeteria. Okay, so it was a metaphorical concussion, but neither my brain nor my heart could tell the difference, and my penis didn't care.

I guess she was wearing clothes.

There are leg men and ass men and breast men. I take turns being all of them. The day she oozed like warm, sinuous, sensuous fog into my life, I became a hip man.

She had bedroom eyes and bedroom hips. She had a wide, red mouth and wide, brown hips. She had a belly like the pillows of oblivion in an opium den, and opulent hips like the divan in a Victorian brothel.

Just watching her sway chickaboomingly across the room, I could tell she could throw you a fuck that would make the devil lose a bargain with a fool. She had hips like God's own business, fuck back atcha hips that could give what she got and come back for more, hips that would make you saddle up and riiiiiide, Jack, and not care where to or how far.

"Whatever you're selling, I'm buying," I assured her from nine feet away.

Without breaking that silken-hipped stride, she beamed, "I'm gonna hold you to that."

By now, I was obliged to get it out of the way. "Do you know who I am?"

"I don't care who you are."

"I'm starting not to myself."

I thought I was snapping a cool cucumber off the vine. "I can be hard to hold, though. I might get away." She was in front of the table. She appraised me critically. My cucumber cooled, and not in a good way.

Then she sat across from me and said, "Just try."

I remember all that distinctly. I have no astonishing level of recollection about the rest, even, as I say, her clothes. Meditating monks can sit for hours or supposedly days seeking nirvana within their own navel.

Hers was better.

My last conscious thought before falling, falling, falling forever into nirvana was her belly button—neither an innie nor an outie but a ribbon of flesh folded flush with her buttery brown belly—as her tummy pouch sank like the last honeyed sun of a golden harvest beneath the contented horizon that was the edge of the table.

She wanted me to murder her husband, I know that. It took her a while to get to that. I smiled and nodded numbly as she led up to it, worked up to it, however it was we got to it.

Something about debuting at a New York hotel, then back to Swiss boarding schools and summering in Biarritz and Saint Tropez. All I could think was this explained the tan as cultivated as a ten-year orchid. What were buzzwords to her were just so much buzzing to me. My brain felt like bees in a hot hive, a mass of amber ooze approaching critical mass near almond orchards and a field of dizzying flowers.

Then I guess it was her MBA at Boston College, which she either did or didn't get, I never settled on which, and off to Martha's Vineyard. I perked up at Martha's, and sank back down into the beebuzz when it wasn't followed by Kitchen.

Oh, and let's see—marrying an up-and-coming broker who was now down and out, before tossing him like a wedding bouquet to the next in line to want him even with his diminished millions: a New York apartment which is still in her name, almost marrying a Senator before leaving him and almost marrying the VP of some three-initialed Fortune 500 company, only to leave *him* and marry the CEO, her Houston husband that she wanted dead.

"Which is why you're perfect for it, darling. And with a hundred thousand dollars, you can just disappear again and everyone will just think you remembered who you are and went there."

The bee reactor reached critical mass. The reaction was self-sustaining, and we had power.

"Who the hell do you think I am?"

"I just told you. You're the guy nobody knows. No fingerprints on file, no—"

"They are *now*," I pointed out.

She patiently re-explained, "Which is why you wear the gloves."

"They'll still think I did it."

"But they won't know who you *are*." She was being very patient and prim, for a clearly insane person talking to a clearly defective one. "They won't even know you've been to Houston."

"They'll know you've been here."

"Not if you don't tell. And for a hundred thousand, you won't."

"I won't have to."

"Then how will anyone know I've been here."

I tilted my hand to her to demonstrate her like a new refrigerator. "You're hard to miss."

She smiled at that. I thought she was going to pat her coiffure, but she didn't. She may as well have.

Without any more movement than straightening up, she preened for the judges. I could almost see the sash.

Her brain didn't even log it. Preening like that was her way of tying her shoelaces.

I brought her back to Earth. "So they'll know you were here."

She brushed it aside. "Darling. In my circles, charity work is *de rigeur.* Wealth has its obligations, and I have a great deal of wealth. I'm simply coming to ask you if there's anything I can do for this Kitchen place. And there clearly is."

"Martha's Kitchen."

"Come again?"

"It's Martha's Kitchen. As in Vineyard."

She smiled at me sweetly.

"It's my home," I explained.

The timer on the smile automatically shut it off. "Of course." She looked around but didn't see anything. "And it's lovely." She flopped a saddlebag purse onto the table. She was wearing, I now noticed, some kind of faux casual, NFL fabulous, chichi-froufrou cowgirl outfit without any tacky fringe, like a cheerleader half her age had traveled into the future and took third in some disco rodeo event. The ensemble included a sort of cowboy hat.

I once dispatched for a towing company. One pompous ass who'd locked his keys in his Mercedes had described its color as "snowpearl white." I had no idea what such a color could look like and wrote white on the ticket. When Manuel, my driver, got back, he laughed and told me how that particular model was a Chrysler redesign of an old Opel power train made from parts milled in South Korea and assembled at a reconditioned Plymouth plant in Windsor, Ontario, Canada. "The only thing Mercedes on that car is the hood ornament and the headlights."

Now I knew what color snowpearl white was. Her cowboy hat was snowpearl white. The hair beneath it had been tinted and coiffed and curled and

straightened and recoiffed and lowlit and highlit and
shellacked until it was snowpearl white, with streaks
of piss.

She had on a snowpearl off-white vest with
white braid piping like a frieze of a thick lasso and a
Prussian blue haltertop. The haltertop had the
luckiest knot that ever existed between her globular
breasts, which jiggled coaxingly even when she was
just sitting there. I suppose she had on either shorts
or a mini skirt, probably.

The boots, I'm guessing, were whatever *de
rigeur* means and some color containing some
combination of the words snow, pearl, and white.

While I'd been taking in her clothes, she'd been
writing a check. The ripping sound was my reverie
coming to an end. I looked at it. Made out to
Martha's Kitchen. Nine grand. New bedding—hell,
new *beds* for the fourth floor. Six months commissary.
Three months electricity. I was having trouble solving
for $x$ on how much pharmacy it could buy.

"Why not ten?"

"Well you're *welcome*," she huffed.

"Look, Miss—" I looked at the check heading: *A
Better Tomorrow, NPO*. I switched to the signature.
*Suki Vanderwaal-McCarthy* "—McCarthy."

"*Missus* McCarthy." She pinched her lips like a
notary seal into a smug smile. I rolled my eyes and
she squeezed my wrist and riled up the bees again.
"For the time being. Think about it. We'll hammer out
the details tomorrow when we do lunch." Her bony
claw hadn't left my wrist. As of my writing this at
six-eighteen tonight, the tingling from her flirtatious
squeeze still hasn't left my wrist.

She squeezed again by way of confirmation,
gathered up her sleek, elegant checkbook portfolio
thingie, and stood up to repack her saddlebag purse.
I'll let you tell me what color it was.

Slinging it onto her shoulder and tossing her
hair at the same time, she stood with her boots apart
and seemed to suck my hand into hers with the

motion of pushing it at me. "It was lovely meeting you."

Then she cranked up those hips again and walked out the door, her world secure and all problems already solved.

Did I mention she had great hips?

Not all of the behaviors I was expected to comply with were on that half-sheet of paper. Most of them weren't. The half-sheet was more of a list of categories. Specific behaviors—some written, some not, a few arbitrary, most common sense if you thought about it—were numerous. Residents and overnight guests who may or may not eventually seek resident status were expected to know all of them.

With the bees gone from my brain and a few still buzzing in the wrist she'd squeezed, I violated the one rule those living on society's undocumented fringe should never even have to mention.

I called Detective Dan Petrucha and snitched.

He wanted me to wear a wire.

I had my digital recorder that Dr. Olverstedt had given me. That was good enough. Dan said there'd be several meetings and I was just to let her talk. I was to play hard to get. Like anyone could be hard for her to get.

"I think I can handle the hard part," I offered.

"I don't want to think about you handling your hard parts."

"Fair enough."

"I'll get in contact with the District Attorneys here and in Houston. Is there any way you could stretch this out till we can get the team assembled? I don't want you meeting her tomorrow."

"I don't think I had a choice. She acted like we already met tomorrow."

"That's some trick."

"Like I'd already killed her husband and we were just debriefing."

"I know the type. It's almost hypnotic."
Whatever Dan said next was blurred out by my
thinking of hips. "You there?"

"I am soooo there," I sighed dreamily.

He sighed. "I'll call you tomorrow."

The next day, he said, "Good news, we don't
think she's dangerous."

"She wants to *kill* the guy, but not
dangerously?"

"To you. She's not dangerous to you. She needs
you alive until he's not alive, at least."

"What if I tell her no, how dangerous is she
gonna be then, to me?

"Hey you're the one who has to meet her
today. Don't tell her no and we won't find out. "

"You told me to play hard to get."

"Hard to get. No is impossible to get. Just for
God's sake do not let her go scampering to find
someone else. We need to build this case long term."

Sagely, I told him, "Rome *was,* however,
burrrrrned in a day."

There was silence on the other end. "Hello?"

Finally, Detective Dan said, "I don't think
whatever brain damage you got caused this. I think
you were always this weird. You really need to learn
to connect a few more dots with folks. Not everybody
can keep up."

"You're actually gonna let me do this?"

"I'm not gonna let you do anything. I could
arrest you for your own good, protective custody. And
I probably should. But Harris County DA wants this
bitch bad. Henry McCarthy always backs the guy who
wins the election, you know. Hundred percent, this
guy."

I said, "Neat trick. What's his secret?"

"You are naive. He just buys everybody that
runs and cashes in the winning ticket."

"Wish I had deep pockets."

"Don't we all. General consensus is, we have no
proof that she's done anything illegal, ever. And she

gave MK a nine-thousand-dollar alibi. It's probably better that you're meeting her without the team this first time. She sniffs anything and scoots, we ain't got a bitch-ass thing."

It's hard to be rueful over the phone. "And, like you say, she's not dangerous. To me. For now."

"We think not."

"And then Decartes vanished in a puff of smoke."

"What?"

"Old joke," I muttered.

"You're weird, dude. What's Decar—oh, I get it." He sighed. "Here's the plan. She talks, you smile and nod."

"Am I still weird?"

"Just be careful."

"But am I weird?" He was gone. "Guess I'll never know."

She called for me at eleven-thirty. Just hearing her voice and knowing those hips were on the other end of the phone line made me dizzy. I hadn't wanted to know my own *name* that bad, that's how bad I wanted her.

We ate. She described charity work, which was mainly calling all the other executive housewives pretending to assuage their boredom with *noblesse oblige* and writing checks to each other's charities or promising to go to each other's luncheons and slave auctions and tennis tournaments and write checks there.

We went somewhere else for coffee and dessert. She explained more about the intricate mechanisms of doing good deeds as a means of not having to interact with their husbands or interfere with their work.

We drove around. Not even the hood ornament and the headlights were Mercedes. They were Jaguar.

All I could think was her skirt suit was decorous orange and that her decorous hips beneath it were decorous brown that went good with orange.

We stopped at a couple of parks and talked with the Jaguar purring cool air at us. I was glad I'd brought my jacket. We chatted, in the pre-internet sense of the word. She chatted. I listened and was glad the digital recorder could hold up to seven hours of conversation. So far, even I knew the cops couldn't hold *her* on any of her conversation.

I was also glad I didn't have a tape I had to figure out how to turn over without her knowing.

Finally, at Tanglefoot Lake Park, we got out and strolled. Lunch had been six stops ago. I was getting hungry again. She hooked her arm in mine and we strolled the shoreline. I felt like my own grandfather strolling with his bride of sixty years. Also, I wanted to bend her over that Jaguar and slamfuck her hard, fast and furious, then tuck my pot belly into the small of her back and listen to her do some purring of her own.

Instead, we strolled, all romance and no sappiness to any viewers about.

"And so," she purred after a long silence. We kept strolling.

"And so." Stroll, stroll, stroll.

"And so, can I count on your support?"

"The only money I have for your charity is none of the nine thousand you gave to mine."

"To do the deed."

"You mean the dead deed."

She stopped strolling. Her arm came out of mine. We squared off. "What we talked about yesterday."

"What *you* talked about yesterday."

She put a hand on each of my biceps. "Can. I count. On your. Support?" She smiled at me sweetly and tilted her head. I think I heard her shellacked curls rattle. Or maybe it was my heart. Throat cartilage around the larynx can rattle like that.

I took her hand and a deep breath, then turned and took her strolling again.

"You knooooow, if you smoke *too* much crack, you'll burn your lips and lose your house."

She hugged my arm and kissed my bicep with her ear. But we kept strolling.

"I'd rather burn my bridges and lose my husband."

"You're quick," I admitted. "Which is why I'm wondering why you're so slow about getting this done, you want it so bad."

Still hugging my arm, she shrugged into it and explained, "There's slow and there's careful."

"Why weren't you slow and careful yesterday?" I'd been wondering this all night and morning.

She turned in exasperated disgust, though I don't think at me. "I'm tired of this. And I'm tired of waiting. This started out as a yes or no question." She shifted metaphorical gears and came around the block again. "Because it's fifty-fifty you're a good person, and even if you are, it's fifty-fifty if you'll remember your morals." Here she came again, answering my question another time. "Because maybe it's just good timing. Maybe it's because you're a ghost in the graveyard, a nobody nobody knows and nobody'll know where you'll head out when you blow town." She quickly reached out and stroked the bicep her ear had been kissing. "I don't mean nobody as in nothing, I—"

I nodded to dismiss her mercenary apology. She went further and tried to soften it.

"Maybe I was waiting for you all along and now you're here and it's time to move. You said you're buying whatever. Well, this is what I'm selling. You still buying?"

I gave this due consideration. Finally, I told her. "I don't know."

She bit back her bile and shook her head for three seconds before she spat, "Pussies. You're all a bunch of pussies. You don't *deserve* cocks if you're not gonna have the balls along with 'em."

"I don't know is better than just no, isn't it?"

She threw her arms up and sighed heavily. "Not much. I'm still hanging by my tits on this one."

Before I knew it, I snapped back, "You kiss your mother with that mouth?"

She could and did emasculate me with an eye-roll. "What? Really? *That's* your big comeback? Yeah, Mr. Phantom. Not only do I kiss my mom, we're *fucking.* Okay?" Another emasculatory eye-roll and the dismissive headshake. "Jesus. Kiss my mother. Kiss my *ass,* is where we're going."

I squeezed my voice into the befuddled hillbilly tenor zone and squeaked, "What would something like that cost?"

She could keep up. "*You?* Three-fifty. Just the cheeks, no tongue."

Now I rattled my voice in a can of destitute black man. "Lemme git tree fiddy."

She didn't bite. Instead, she said bitingly, "Yes or no, Ace. Clock's ticking."

"I'm not sure, but I think I once got some good advice. When it's take it or leave it, leave it."

"I'm not saying take it or leave it, I'm saying take it and leave town."

"Take the money and run." I almost sang it.

She nodded. "Far, far away."

I considered. I had to admit it: "I still don't know."

She threw her hands up again. "Gee-zus. If I had a gun right now I'd kill you myself, and *fuck* my husband."

"I thought it was your mother you were fucking."

"Stop. With. The games. And deal. With the issue. At hand."

"Do you really have sex with your mother?"

"No!"

"Because that's kinda kinky."

She sighed so hard it physically deflated her. "Why are you *mocking* me with this?" She began slowly shaking her head and talking into both collar bones. "All I wanted was to kill my husband. Seemed simple enough, on the face. Total stranger, one shot, gun in the channel, even a car to leave town in. Hundred grand, who couldn't disappear with a hundred grand? But noooo, I get some hobo *clown* whose only cleverness is in his tongue and who's only a man in name only, with *zero* balls to speak of, why?" Then she looked to me for an answer.

"Well casting aspersions on my manhood won't help," I pouted.

She was choking on spittle and consternation. "Casting asper—? Well I *guess* I know what that word means, unless you just made it up in your Mr. Crazytime brain."

"Now it's my *sanity*. I have a *brain glitch*. A glitch in my brain. The rest of me works just fine."

She looked with ill-contained loathing at her husband back in Houston and gripped my biceps again. "The man. Deserves. To die. And *you*"—she shoved me away—"get me so fucked around I'm forgetting him and wishing you deserved to die instead. Now answer. My fucking. Question.

"I don't *know*," I surrendered, palms up. Maybe I sighed a little too. "I don't know." Her head dropped in futility, as from a guillotine, but I pressed on. "I don't know, Suki. Besides a threesome, every man's most persistent fantasy is to completely erase his identity and completely disappear." I looked at her. She swallowed and regrouped.

"And we can make that fantasy happen," she nudged patiently.

"Except, it's already happened. I've already disappeared. Far as the world's concerned, my entire past has been etch-a-sketched." I shook my jowls as a visual aid. "So I don't need you. Unless..."

She looked her question at me. I said, "Unless you were talking about the threesome fantasy."

"No I was *not* talking about making the threesome fantasy happen. Is that *really* all you men think women are good for?"

"No, of course not," I automatically responded.

Then it hit me. I faced her head on for the first time. "But it's all some women are good for."

We let that sit between us like a gun on the table. I was daring her to pick it up and pull that trigger. She was refusing to believe I was daring her to pull that particular trigger.

"So you're saying..." she attempted.

I paused, deliberately. I nodded, deliberately.

She refused. "Fuck me," she huffed hopelessly. "Fuck my fucking fucked self." The challenge made her head lift. "You'll kill my husband if I—"

"Yes," I finished when she couldn't. She began shaking her head in denial of it all and I added, "We have sex, you're a widow."

"My *mother* has a better shot than you."

I shrugged. God, it felt good. "Then you and Prince Charming live"—I let it drip like honey —"happilyyyyy everrrr afterrrr."

"You're serious. You're actually—that's your actual and for real price."

I pinched my lips together. This time it didn't drip. "Yes. Yes, I believe it is."

"How many times?"

I smirked. "Depends on how good it is."

"Oh fuck *you,* Kitchen boy. How about I blow you, and the money?"

"How about we find a hotel, and eight hours later you're sore and sticky. *And* the money."

"How about you shove the gun up your ass and pull the trigger? Sore and sticky!"

"And they lived happily ever after."

"Stop *saying* that," she screeched. "Christ, you're a sick bastard."

"I'm a healthy bastard. With a healthy sex drive. And I can't *remember* the last time I got laid. Literally."

"Well it's easy to see why. Let me explain something to you, Scooter. This is million-*dollar* cooch. Fat old men with ten-digit trust funds fuck over entire *companies* just so they can afford the *ticket* on this ride."

"Maybe mine goes to eleven," I offered.

She raised one contemptuous eyebrow. "I'd like to *see* the day you could sport eleven. You and your eight hours later. Maybe in the metric system."

"Well, I was talking about my trust fund."

"Pesos? Lira? Oh right, they don't have lira anymore. Like your trust fund. Because maybe I'm thinking eleven *dollars* if you're lucky." She snorted. "Eleven."

"Well that's the thing. I don't know. Nobody knows. *Could be meat. Could be cake.*"

She squinted as she snorted a confused, "Hh-*what?*"

"Maybe I'm rich too. Maybe I'm fantastically adept in bed. If nothing else, you said I'm clever with my tongue."

"And blind as a shithouse *mole*. You have *no* idea, *none,* how much sex I *don't* want to have with you. You can't even see the taillights on this one, buddy."

I smiled slyly. "Aren't taillights always red?"

She caught her lower lip as she was cranking up the F in fuck you. Instead, she chomped off the expletive and spat, "So now I'm a whore?"

"Ten digits, eleven pesos, now we're just haggling over the price."

"The answer is no."

I smiled helplessly and conceded, "It certainly is."

"No," she asserted.

"Yes. No. My answer is no."

"You can't *do* this to me."

"Apparently not," I smirked.

"You *dick.*" She gathered steam. "Calling me a whore? A whore? Casting *asper-gins*. This is how you woo your women? Let me tell you, with me, you'd remember it even if you forgot *English*. You shitball dickwad, but I gotta waste it on you just to put my husband out of his misery? Fuck that. And fuck you. You won't tell me no, but I'm a whore to you? Fuck *your* mother, dickhole."

"Depends on how bad you want him dead, I guess."

She downshifted into the conversational curve. "Look, sweetie. Your morals are kicking in, I can see that. Okay. You're on the wire with this. It's a scary thought, I know. But you're scared to tell me no, so you work the sex angle, knowing I'll kick. I'll tell you no, instead. I can see that. Mamma understands. But trying to force me into bed is just gonna make sure *nobody* gets well off this, don't you see?"

I was looking at the lakeshore sand. She may have touched my arm again.

"Now, the pussy's off the table. That will remain the golden unattainable. Hundred grand, I'll blow you if that'll seal the deal and I can keep from retching. But you gotta know, you have to know you can't just wade hip deep into all this and then back out. Even just talking about it, you're up to your nuts in shit. Might as well hold your nose and duck under, and it'll all be over with soon."

I thought, "I could give you the same advice," but didn't say it.

I looked at her a long time. "I think I'm already in over my head."

"That's the spirit," she chirped. "Now just swim as fast as you can for the far shore and let's do this puppy."

"I—honestly? I can't. Whatever I am, I'm not that. I can't."

("This is how he *doesn't* tell her no?" Detective Pitrucha said when he heard the digital recording.)

"...useless *bastard.* You're gonna leave me twisting in the wind on this? I expose *everything* of myself to you and *then* you decide I'm some shitty diaper you leave in the Walmart restroom? Huh? Don't you understand, I *need* you."

"I can't."

"What do you *mean* you can't? You *have* to."

I shook my head. I don't think she even saw a boat sailing out of the bay without ever knowing she was on the island. She kept going. "You're *in* this, buddy. You don't help me out, I've gotta find somebody to kill you so I'm not looking over my shoulder all my days."

"No you don't."

"Yes I *will*. I'll *have* to."

"Look," I placated. "None of this has to happen. Go home, get a divorce"—I squashed her interruption at its gasp stage and kept shoving—"take the prenup money and live happily every after *that* way." She was refusing even the possibility, but I still kept shoving it home. "Suki, you're, you're more than smart. You are fucking *beyond* beautiful. You've been in the show long enough to play off any leading man, just pick one and go at it."

"Nooo." She began to cry without knowing it.

"Yes. You can do it. You've done it since you left Switzerland, with nothing but that Fifth Avenue Apartment. You don't need *all* the money, and you don't need to out and out kill some defenseless bastard just for having it. If he's as old as you say he is, just serving the papers'll probably kill him."

"You don't understand," she wailed breathily.

"I don't have to understand. And neither do you. Just find a pit bull lawyer with nothing to lose and pay *him* the hundred grand."

"Useless," she moaned. "All of it."

I hammered another nail. "You're not a killer. You're not. And even if you are, I'm not. But you are not. Find a killer lawyer, a whole shark school, and be as vicious as you want. But leave me out of it. Whoever I am, I'm not the guy for this. Not this. I'm not the guy for any of this, okay?"

She sighed through her nose and couldn't face me. "I could kill me. Then no one would be involved."

I measured her for a minute. "That's not you either, and you know it."

She clenched her fists in frustration. "Nothing fucking works on you, does it?"

What could I say? So I didn't say it.

"Fine. I'll fuck you. Best pussy in the land, it's yours, just get him out of my life."

"Dammit, woman, I can't. I can't, I can't, I *just flat-out can't.* It's not me. Something in me says no, and it's not gonna change."

"What do you *waaant?*" she screamed. It hurt my throat in sympathy for hers more than it hurt hers. She beat the air, instead of my face which wouldn't help her.

"Why are you throwing this on me? You want your answer, it's no. If it's not the answer you were looking for, it's not my fault."

That got her. I withstood the icy glare, but I don't think I could again.

"No, as long as it's not your fault, it's all okay, isn't it? Fuck me and roll off, but it's not your fault, so the heavens are in order. Fuck you for getting all sanctimonious over this."

"How am I being—?"

"How *dare* you. You were waiting to bend me over that stupid chair in your *cafeteria,* weren't you? You were wanting bad to fuck me, and when you figured you couldn't, you fucked me instead. I hope you pull your cock off in midstroke and fuck your own *eye.*"

"*Wow,*" I flailed, as if that had actually happened.

"I'd like to rip your nutsack off and slap you with it like a bag of donuts, you weaselly little shit."

"Okay. Now you are *offically* in the psycho zone, lady. Maybe you should—"

"Just fuck *youuu,*" she screeched. There went our throats again.

"Well fuck you too, you crazy bitch," I snapped. "Get out of here."

But she was already leaving. I watched.

It took me seven minutes before my breath stopped being a bull's snort and my heart stopped warping my temples so I looked like one of those Squeezit stress heads.

I looked around. There was no one to ask, but I had to anyway. "Did that just—did that just *happen?*"

I'm sure the trees answered by nodding sagely, but there wasn't an answer in the world that could convince me that it had.

Even with the seven-mile walk back to Martha's Kitchen, I wasn't entirely back to normal when I got there. Dr. Olverstedt planted her stubby legs in front of mine and hooked her hand under my chin until I looked up at her. "You look like two miles of bad road."

"Tanglefoot Lake Park to here."

"That's seven miles of bad road. You walked?"

"Had to. I remembered how to hitchhike, but nobody remembered to pick me up."

She put her palm on my cheek.

"I have a fever?" I smiled.

She switched to my forehead. After a minute. "No. Just a seven-mile flush."

"Bad road," I agreed.

"Hey. You okay?"

Grateful, I nodded. "Full disclosure, I am scuffed up a bit, all in all. Few skid marks on my heart. But I'll live. Right now, I wish I wouldn't, but I'll live."

I took a shower and a nap, which was against the rules but all they could do is throw me out. At least I could nap until they did.

Instead, I napped until Detective Dan called. I briefly briefed him and tried to nap again, but it was only forty minutes till curfew so I listened to the digital recording.

The next day, Dr. Olverstedt and I took turns transcribing it, with me also adding the stuff you didn't hear. Then we took it all to Dan and he took it all to the various DA's involved.

*Submitter's Note: The man known to the staff, residents and guests here at Martha's Kitchen variously as Ray, Lee Ray, X-ray, Former Lee Ray, Professor X and No Name was brutally murdered in Tanglefoot Lake Park six months and three days after his recorded meeting with Suki Vanderwaal-McCarthy. His hands were chopped off. Detective Sergeant Daniel Petrucha speculates the intention was to leave his fingerprints at the murder scene of William Henry McCarthy less than twelve hours later, though for whatever reason, this was not done.*

*Ray had been frequenting Tanglefoot Lake Park, explaining in an unusually succinct way that at least there he had "something to remember." Before either body was discovered (Ray's not until after three days of an exhaustive search), in fact two days before the murders took place, Suki boarded a plane for Mexico City, from there traveling by chartered jet to Venezuela, which honors no extradition treaty with the US. To date, Ray's true identity has not surfaced. He is buried in a simple grave under the inscription "Nameless Friend."*

Signed *(illegibly)*, Dr. Hannah Olverstedt , DO

# ILLEGAL ALIENS

*by G. Lloyd Helm*

Big Dave and I tended to change bars every so often. We'd get bored or something would happen and we'd get eighty-sixed or the bar would suddenly disappear like The Hole in the Wall or Mickey's Mouse Hole, but mostly we would just go looking for adventure at different places, which was how we ended up at the Windy City Saloon out in Mojave.

I had found the Windy City on a trip through the city of Mojave during a time I lived at Edwards Air Force Base with my wife Master Sergeant Michele Helm. That was about the same time I first met Big Dave Dodge at the Hole in the Wall Bar which was out in the desert from Edwards. That meeting turned out to lead to interesting things, like running across, and running away from the ghost of Tiburcio Vasquez the Mexican bandit, and later discovering where Walt Disney was really buried, or stored like a popsicle really.

Now, Big Dave fits the name. 6' 6", 270 lbs. Long hair, long beard, sometimes braided, sometimes not, dressed mostly in leather, denim, and motorcycle boots. He made a good deal of his living with his looks, playing wild bikers in the movies and on TV, but he was in fact not a Hells Angel or a Mongol or affiliated with any such outfit. He was a very gentle giant that made a little of his living writing greeting card poetry. Don't get me wrong, he was no pussy cat. It took a lot to get his dander up, but when it was up he was pretty much a force of nature. I once saw him lift a motorcycle over his head and throw it—granted it was a smallish bike, but still.

Anyway, Dave and I fetched up in the Windy City Saloon because I had told him about my first encounter there. It had been all about the wind and how strong it could get in the Antelope Valley and where it came from. And when I told Dave that I had been assured by people in the Windy City that the wind had once gotten so high as to pick up steel train wheels and fling them over the mountain into Edwards AFB airspace, and set off a panic because the wheels showed up like flying saucers on the Edwards radar, he said, *"Oh ho ho,* this is a joint I gotta see."

Now, the Windy City Saloon doesn't look like much—more hovel than building, but it was pretty much an institution with a wide variety of people. I had met desert rats and cowboys and prospectors and makers of train wheels and some of the most truly colossal liars I had ever run into anywhere, which meant that the conversation in the joint was always lively and interesting, so long as one didn't take it too seriously, or rather knew when to take it seriously and when not.

One evening Dave and I were sitting in the bar sipping beer and watching the TV hung up over in the corner. The thing was turned onto the History Channel or some such—see the Windy City ain't your typical bar with sports or such on the TV. During the baseball season you might catch a Dodgers game or something but most other times the channel stayed on History or National Geographic or one of the other information channels—anyhow, the history channel or something was on and they were talking about UFOs and ancient visitations by extra terrestrial beings and space flights and marks left on walls that were supposed to have been left there by people who had actually had some kind of truck with the aliens when they were here, and when a commercial hit Jimmy, the owner and bar tender of the place, said—"There's a lot of those wall markings around here, ya know?

Over by Barstow at Fort Irwin there's a whole mess of 'em."

"Yeah, and up in the Red Rock country, too." Earl, a regular denizen of the bar chimed in.

"Big cave up out of Tehachapi got lots of 'em, too," I added. "I been up there. Long walk in, though. California State Park Rangers do guided tours up there in the Spring and Fall."

"So what did the wall writing have to say" Dave asked and sucked in a swig of beer.

Clyde, another regular chimed in with, "Pro'bly said, 'Heap big flying saucer come down, et up all the *antelope* in the *valley*.'" This was a standard joke about the lack of antelopes anywhere in the Antelope Valley.

"Ya'll go on and scoff," a fella in stripped overalls and an engineer cap said. "I ain't so sure them ancient alien guys are wrong." I had met him before, but somehow had never caught his name. He was the one that worked in the train wheel factory over on the other side of Mojave who had told us about the train wheels setting off the UFO scramble over at Edwards.

"Awh, you don't believe that shit any more'n I do," Jimmy said

The other fellow shrugged. "Air Force believes it," he said.

"Ah, that's bullshit," Clyde snorted and took a drink of beer.

"I promise ya it ain't, Clyde," I said. "There really is a protocol for UFO sightings. My wife used to have to deal with 'em sometimes when we still lived on base. I 'member once she didn't get back from work for two days because the US of A Air Force was out chasing lights in the sky. I saw 'em too. Half a dozen really bright balls of light looked like they were flying in formation over the base. They came and went a mess of times. Scrambled fighters to chase 'em and everything"

"Bah," Clyde said. "Sun dogs or something."

"I don't know—you could be right. I don't think they ever figured out what that was all about. By and by the balls went away and that was the end of it."

Big Dave had mostly just been sitting and sipping as he listened to the TV and then to the back and forth but now he said, "Maybe the UFOs missed their target. Maybe they were supposed to be doing recon on Area 51."

All of a sudden the bar got quiet. Everybody from around Mojave had heard of Area 51. It was supposed to be a super secret test base for new air planes over in western Nevada and all the ufologists thought there was Extra Terrestrial stuff being hidden and tested over there.

There had been reports, supposedly by people who had worked over there, about flying saucers that scientists and engineers were tearing apart to find out about propulsion systems and skin covering systems and other stuff. There was rumor that the stealth technology that made American fighters invisible to radar had come from what had been discovered in these hidden flying saucers.

People around Mojave and the Antelope Valley in general took anything that had to do with aerospace testing dead serious. The AV and Mojave were home to test flights and reaches into space from the old X-15 and Chuck Yeager to Dick Rutan and SpaceShipOne. Mojave was already advertizing itself as "Spaceport Mojave" on their "Welcome to Town" signs.

After a while good ol' doubting Clyde—who had once told me he had seen wind in the AV so strong that it could scoot an anvil along the ground— chimed in with a snort and said, "Well, if they comin' to invade us we got nothing to worry about, do we? if they can't tell the difference between Edwards, California and Area 51, Nevada."

A bit later on when I was on my way home to Michele I began thinking about the bar conversation.

This was a dangerous thing. A couple of times before I had started thinking about bar conversations, and it had gotten Dave and I into some sticky situations. But Dave wasn't with me so I had no one to talk to about my thoughts, and as I drew closer to home I remembered that last time my thoughts had gotten Dave and I into trouble Michele had promised that I could find someone else to go my bail next time an adventure ended badly, so I closed my thoughts up and did my best to forget about them.

A couple of days passed and, try as I might, curiosity about Area 51 kept pricking my mind like a tiny hair splinter will prick your finger when you rub it just a certain way. But I didn't let the thoughts get out of hand like I had the wonderation about Disney which had landed me and big Dave and a couple of other people in the LA County Lockup for a couple of days. But I am convinced that the Universe or God or something has a great deal to say about these things because just when I thought I had gotten control of the Area 51 fever Michele got a call from her sister. Now, Michele's sister's life has been a soap opera ever since I have known her, but there had been a sudden uptick of the soap, leaving Sis aground and in need of comfort, so Michele packed an overnight bag and headed for Simi with a simple, "I'll be back in a couple of days. Stay out of trouble," and she was gone. The vibration of the closing door had hardly stopped when the phone rang. It was Dave.

"Hey, G," he said. "I just ran across an opportunity that you might like to get in on."

"Oh yeah? What?"

"An outfit name of Willis Pictures is thinking about shooting a low budget sci-fi flick up in the desert near Area 51. I know all those guys and they asked me if I would go up there and scout some locations and shoot some pix around the area, so I said yeah. You wanna come?"

"How you gonna get there? I can't see myself riding bitch on your Harley all the way to Nevada."

He laughed. "Naw. Willis said I could take his car. Lincoln Town Car."

"Ugh, a barge."

"Yeah, but it's a comfortable barge and he's paying for the gas."

"Bar in the back?"

"Yeah, and air conditioning."

I rolled the situation around in my mind for a little while. It sounded really tempting and it made that "wonder" itch start to burn in my chest.

"Michele is out of town," I said. "Gone to her sister's..."

"Then what she doesn't know won't hurt her— or us."

I let that roll around in my mind for a while too and remembered—maybe she didn't really mean she wouldn't go my bail if things went salty. I mean she said she loved me and we had been married for forty years—besides, what could go wrong?

Later that afternoon Dave rolled up in front of the house in a dark green Lincoln land yacht and honked for me.

"Kinda late to be starting this, isn't it?" I said as I got in.

"I guess, but I had the car and the cameras and the gas and it just seemed like we needed to get on with it. It'll be cooler, anyhow."

"I reckon. If it's too late when we get over there I guess we can find a place to crash."

"Hell, big as this thing is we can crash right here in the car. You take the back seat and I'll take the front."

I glanced to the back seat and saw that he was probably right. I'm sure there are whole Asian families that grow up with less space.

We drove along in silence for a while just watching the Joshua trees go by heading north-east up old US 395. We could have cut a more direct route across Death Valley but neither of us wanted to get stuck out there in the middle of the night. It was late October so we probably wouldn't have died of thirst but still ... Death Valley. Instead we headed up toward Mono Lake where we could cut across through Tonopah and hit what was called—even on the maps —*The Extraterrestrial Highway*.

"You know anything about this Area 51, Dave?

"Just what I've read and seen on TV."

"You figure there really are flying saucers and little green men up there?"

"I figure if there are they are in cahoots with Big Brother."

I thought about that for a little bit and had to shake my head. "David, I spent twenty two years dealing with the Air Force and other US of A government agencies and couldn't any of 'em keep a secret for shit. All you'd have to do is hang around some of the local watering holes for a couple of days and you'd know everything there was to know about everything happening on the base."

"That reminds me," Dave said. "You got your military ID on you?"

"Always. Why?"

"'Cause your card and my silver tongue are gonna get us on base to have a look around."

"I said you could find out anything by hanging around, but I doubt they are gonna just let us in the gate on the weight of my retired civilian dependant ID card. They're stupid, not *stupid!* if ya know what I mean."

"Reckon we'll find out," he said.

We spent the next several hours looking at the scenery and singing with the radio until it got pretty much too dark to see anything outside the headlights. By then we had crossed into Nevada and passed Tonopah and were looking for the turn off onto Nevada Highway 375. *The Extraterrestrial Highway.* By then it was getting latish and we were both getting tired and thirsty. We turned onto Highway 375 and started the final leg of the trip. The road was not promising as to lodging or food or drink. It was one of those no-lights, total dark, more like driving down a long black tunnel roads. Nothing seeable along the sides until there suddenly was something to see. The headlights washed over two guys beside the road with their thumbs stuck up.

Now myself, I had hitchhiked a few thousand miles in the US when I was a kid, and when we were stationed in Europe the whole family had hitched around in times we had no car, but since I have gotten a little older I've gotten a little more cynical—or maybe scared. I couldn't remember the last time I had hitched a ride, but more importantly I couldn't remember the last time I had picked up a hitchhiker.

The hitchhikers surprised Dave too, so much that he let out a big "Holy..." and whipped the car away toward the middle of the road while stomping on the brakes hard enough to squeal and smoke the tires.

By the time we got stopped the two hitchhikers were standing beside the car. It takes a long time to stop a big old Lincoln Town Car, but, now that I think about it, it still seems like they got to the car pretty fast, but anyhow there they were. A couple of Air Force guys—an A1C and a Senior Airman—in blues and fore and aft caps.

"You guys OK?" they were asking, their voices muffled by the closed windows and the humming air conditioning. I rolled down my window and they asked again if we were OK.

"You guys just scared the shit out of us, popping out of the dark like that. What the hell are you doing out here in the middle of nowhere?" I asked

"That's a long sad story I don't even want to go into," the Senior Airman said.

"Sounds like it involves women," Dave said.

The A1C let out a kind of pitiful groan and the Senior said, "Please."

Dave and I both laughed. "Where you headed?" I asked.

"Back to the base, to lick our wounds in solitude." The Senior said.

"Would that be Area 51 kinda base?" Dave asked.

"Yeah."

"You guys work over there?"

"Hey, then you are just the guys we'd like to talk to."

Dave's words struck these guys almost like he had hit them with a shovel or something. They both hung their heads and shook them in gestures of negation. "More flying saucer chasers," the A1C said.

"Ah come on, guys," I said. "We are just out here scouting locations for a movie..."

"A zombie movie," Dave said. "Zombies from outer space."

This was the first I had heard about zombies so I figured Dave was making it up as he went along, but I was willing so what the hell...

"Yeah," I said "and since you guys are stationed around here I bet you know some great places for zombie massacres and stuff..."

"And we'd even buy ya a beer in return for the information," Dave said. "If there's any place to buy beer out here."

That seemed to perk them up some. "I could use a beer, for sure," the Senior said.

"Great," Dave said. "Where we going?"

"That way," the A1C said, pointing up the road toward Area 51. "Only joint along here is the Spaceship Bar and Grill just outside the base gate."

"*Spaceship Bar and Grill?*" I thought, and the thought sent a shiver down my spine.

The joint was aptly named. It was a cinder block building which had a sheet metal facade over the front. Above the building was a long skinny antenna with a red ball on top and over the entrance was a red and blue blinky sign that said Spaceship Bar and Grill.

The place wasn't exactly jumping. I didn't see another car in the dirt parking lot, and as I thought about it I didn't remember any cars passing us as we moved down the road. Area 51 was pretty much out in the toolies, but I figured a base as famous as Area 51 would have at least some traffic going in and out. But it was pretty late, so I didn't think about it much. I was tired and thirsty and ready to curl up in the back seat of the land yacht and cop a couple of Zs.

We got out and headed up the ramp that looked like a big silver tongue lapping out of the front of the bar ... and that is the last thing I remember—I mean really remember. I have some vague memories like the rags of a dream that didn't make any sense at all. Flash pictures of people leaning over me, but not exactly people. More like gray blobs with big black eyes and slit nostrils. And I remember being cold because I seemed to be naked on some kind of a steel table.

And then it was morning. I woke up stretched out in the back seat of the Lincoln with what felt like the worst hangover I have ever endured. Throbbing head, throbbing nasty stomach, throbbing anal sphincter like I had just gone through a colonoscopy. I was almost afraid to move for fear something might fall off and bring on wider disaster.

"Dave," I said. It came out kind of a croak. My voice was rusty-crusty like after a lot of hollering at a ball game. I cleared my throat and tried again. "Dave."

"Whaaa?" he answered from the front seat.

"What happened?"

"Whaaa?"

"I am hung over like a big dog," I said. "Wha'd ya let me drink so much for?"

"Let ya drink? I don't remember drinking nothin'."

A knock on the window scared us both. It was a couple of Air Force Security cops complete with gleaming bloused boots, blue berets and M16s. They weren't aimed at us but they were in a position where they could be without too much difficulty.

"Out of the car," one of 'em commanded.

I managed to sit up without my head exploding, but it was a near thing, and when I bent a little to pull up the lock knob on the door there was a real danger of something else exploding, but I held it down thinking it probably wouldn't help my case any if I barfed on the cops' shiny boots.

Dave appeared to be having the same trouble which was why the cop could spin him around into the classic pat down position without resistance. I had never seen anybody manhandle Big Dave like that and I had always figured that if anyone tried it they were in for trouble. Like I said, Dave was mostly a gentle giant, but he had his limits.

My cop spun me around and I just sorta naturally assumed the position, leaning against the car. Now, I've been frisked before, but it seemed like this guy was enjoying it more than he should have. I sure wasn't. The third time he bashed/squeezed my jewels I was considering swinging around and puking on those shiny boots just to get even.

By and by the SPs seemed satisfied that we weren't armed so they spun us back around and asked, "What the hell are you people doing here?"

"We ain't doing anything officer," I started out. "Just sleeping in the car. That isn't against the law, is it?"

"It is if you're sitting just outside the gate of a military facility," Dave's cop said. "Bombs and terrorist attacks and stuff," he went on as though talking to a three year old.

"We got no bombs or bad intentions," Dave said. "We just stopped here to have a beer with a couple airmen we picked up hitchhiking."

"Stopped for a beer?" my cop said, doubt clear in his voice.

"Yeah," I said, a bit more crankily than I probably should have. "Just go in and ask the bar..." I hooked a thumb back over my shoulder at the Spaceship Bar and Grill, but as I did I turned my head a little and noticed that Dave was turned completely around and facing the bar with this astonished look on his face. I turned on around and probably got that same astonished look since there was no building or any sign that there had ever been a building there.

"There was a bar there last night, Officer," I said. "Kind of a crappy looking place with a neon sign that said Spaceship Bar and Grill. Even kinda looked like a flying saucer."

The SP didn't look convinced. He looked at his partner and at Dave who said, "Honest to God, Officer, he's telling the truth. It was right there."

"Uh huh," Dave's SP said, not sounding at all convinced. "OK, turn around and put your hands behind you—both of you."

I glanced at the M16 but didn't even consider doing anything but what I was told. In moments we were handcuffed and sitting in the back seat of a blue and white hummer.

"Boy, I hope Michele was kidding about just leaving me sit in the slammer if I got sent there again," I whispered to Dave.

The SPs drove us past the gate guard shack and right onto the base. Area 51 was right in front of us, but there wasn't a whole lot to see. Just more desert. I figured the hangars and flight line were the other side of a rise of hills that was just off to our left. We had wanted to get onto the base—well, we had succeeded admirably, much to our dismay.

We followed the black-topped road until we came to a small group of buildings. We still couldn't see the flight line, but we could see the big blue and white sign that said 96<sup>th</sup> Security Police Squadron. Our captors parked in front and marched us in the door and into a holding cell. They uncuffed us and went through the whole schmear of taking our belts and shoelaces just to make sure we didn't do ourselves serious hurt and I thought about Arlo Gutherie and Alice's Restaurant.

Over the next several hours we were questioned by first a Master Sergeant, then a Captain and finally by a Colonel. We told them all the same story about coming to shoot location pix and picking up the two hitchhiking Airmen and stopping at the bar that was no longer there and not remembering how we got back in the Lincoln or anything else until the SPs knocked on the window this morning. We swore repeatedly that we weren't UFO hunters or Area 51 watchers, but it didn't seem to do any good. Nobody believed us.

After hours of questions and answers they delivered us some food and drink on stainless steel trays and that did not bode well.

"Good thing Michele is out of town," Dave said, "'cause it looks like they are gonna keep us for the night anyhow."

"You got anyone you can call to get us out of here?"

"I got a lawyer friend, but in case you hadn't noticed, we haven't been offered our phone call. We are being held incommunicado, which is illegal, or was until 'Homeland Security' got power to tap phones without warrants and stuff. We may end up in Cuba for all I know."

I swallowed hard. "You don't really think they'd do that, do you?"

He shrugged. "Wouldn't think so, but as crazy as everything else has been, who knows?"

We sat and pretended to eat and thought our own thoughts for a while, then Dave asked, "What do you remember about last night?"

"Just what I been telling the cops. Same as you."

"Do you remember actually going into the bar, or what ever it was?"

I rolled that question around in my mind for a while before answering, "No. I remember getting out of the car and walking up that ramp thing that looked like a big tongue hanging out the front door but that is the last I really remember."

"Yeah, me too. Did you dream while we were asleep in the Lincoln?"

"Not really. Vague stuff. Big headed people with big black eyes and being cold and scared, but not able to really do anything about it."

"Me too. I'm beginning to wonder if maybe those Airmen we picked up weren't exactly what they seemed," Dave said with an ironic lift of an eyebrow.

By and by they came and pulled us out of the holding cell and put us into a cell with bunks. That did not make me feel any better but at least they left us together. Now, a steel box bunk is not comfortable at the best of times, but when you don't have the slightest idea what is gonna happen next it is even more uncomfortable. Nevertheless, I managed to sleep a little and I guess Dave did too because we both had to be shaken awake in the morning.

Our alarm clock was a guy in a gray suit that looked as though he had slept in it. He needed a hair cut and could have used a little mouthwash, but I remembered I was still in custody so I kept my mouth shut.

"Who are you?" Dave asked

"Bob Jones. I want to ask you a couple of questions."

"Go ask the SPs," Dave said. "They got all the answers we could give 'em, and I'm tired of repeating myself."

Brother Jones was sorta taken aback and glanced from Dave to me, but I had nothing to say so he turned and called out, 'Airman...'"

A uniformed Airman SP came and opened the cell door. Brother Jones said, "You guys want some coffee? Maybe some breakfast?" sounding very friendly.

Dave and I glanced at each other with a *what the hell?* kind of look, but we got up and followed Jones out and into what looked like a break room where steaming cups of coffee were already waiting for us.

We sat down and cautiously sipped the coffee, which wasn't awful.

"I know you guys have told your story a hundred times already," Jones began, "but if you'll humor me by telling it one last time maybe we can get you out of here and on your way again."

That sounded good to me so I told him just what we had told everyone else.

When I shut up Dave said, "Just who are you, Bob? Not Air Force, I'd guess, and I'd bet my last nickel your name ain't Jones either, so just who are you? CIA? NSA? "

Jones lifted an eyebrow, no doubt considering whether to simply stick us back in our cell and leave us to rot, but after a little he said, "I'm ETLO. Part of Project Blue Book."

"Blue Book?" I said. "I thought Blue Book was long gone."

"Only parts of it."

"You're here to find out if we were really kidnapped by little green men," Dave said.

"And to debrief us about it."

Jones shrugged. "More or less."

"What does ETLO stand for?" I asked.

"Extraterrestrial Liaison Office," he said. "Now, if I could have your version of what happened, Mr. Dodge?"

Jones listened and questioned us for a couple more hours as we told basically the same story again. "Why do you think they chose you?" he asked.

"I think we just happened to come along," Dave said. "They were just like some naturalist out tagging wolves to study their hunting habits. They grabbed us because we came into their sights."

"Do you think they 'tagged' you?"

"Maybe. There have been reports of other people who have been 'taken' finding odd little metal pellets under their skin and stuff. They might have put some kind of device up my ass."

"Yeah," I added. "I sorta felt like I'd had a colonoscopy when I woke up."

Jones nodded. "Would you consider allowing us to fluoroscope you to see if they did tag you?" he asked.

Dave and I looked at one another and finally Dave shrugged. "Sure, why not, so long as it gets us out of here."

After they X-rayed us they turned the Lincoln and the cameras back over to us and escorted us out the same gate we had come in, making sure we didn't stray between the clinic and the front gate. We pulled into the lot were the Spaceship Bar and Grill had been and the blue and white SP hummer pulled in right behind us.

"OK, now what, Dave?"

"Now we do what we came here to do, take location pix—starting with an open lot where a spaceship landed." He reached into the back seat and pulled up a camera, then got out. I had my doubts that the SPs would let us take a picture so close to the gate, and when Dave got out with the camera the SPs, armed with their M16s, got out and stood beside their hummer, but they didn't interfere as Dave shot several pix of the lot and the open desert around it. He did make sure not to aim at the cops or at the

gate and when he was finished he got back in the car
as did the cops.

"OK," I said, and noticed that I had been
holding my breath. "Can we go now?"

Dave grinned at me. "What'sa matter, G? You
nervous?"

"Nervous? *Bugger all!* Nervous! Will you just
drive, already?"

He laughed and hit the gas, leaving the cops
and their hummer in a cloud of dust.

I figured we were on our way back to
Lancaster, but I was wrong. We got down the
Extraterrestrial Highway a few miles when Dave
pulled to the side of the road. A dirt road led off into
the desert toward a line of bluing hills in the
distance.

"What's up?" I asked.

"I promised Willis I'd shoot some pix and I'm
gonna do it."

I got the distinct impression that there was
more to it than that. "You really think that's a good
idea in view of what we just went through?"

"Sure, what the hell? What else could happen?"

I shook my head and thought back to a lesson
I had learned so long ago I had forgotten when.
"David," I began, "never, ever, under any circumstance
dare worse."

He studied me for a moment, but finally said,
"Ahh. We're just gonna take some pix. That's all."

I didn't believe a word of it, but I was willing
to back Dave up in about anything so I said, "OK.
Drive on." He narrowed his eyes quizzically at me
again, but after a moment he completed the turn onto
the dirt track and we were off.

Now, I don't know that Dave was actually
setting out to find the Spaceship Bar and Grill again,
and if he had intended to find it, how the hell he
accomplished it I don't know either, but we had gone
down that dusty desert track about five miles when I
saw the sun glinting off something in the distance.

That sun glare made my stomach turn over, but I kept my mouth shut, telling myself that it couldn't possibly be what I was afraid it was. Dave didn't say anything, just kept driving and after a bit, there among the creosote and grease wood bushes was the Spaceship Bar and Grill, or at least the spaceship that might once have been disguised as a bar. Now there was no blinky sign and no tongue-looking ramp flapped out the front. This was a largish silver disk, domed on top, that was maybe forty feet tall and a hundred feet in diameter. It was sitting on three stubby legs like the legs on the bottom of an Aladdin lamp. It wasn't whirling or blinking or anything, it just sat there in the desert brush looking incongruous. No one was stirring around the disk, not even a mouse or a jack rabbit.

Dave stopped the land yacht right in the middle of the road, picked up the camera that had been sitting between us and rolled out his door. I wasn't convinced that was the best course of action, but like I said, I usually back Dave up in pretty much everything.

"Get the other camera, G," he said snapping pix of the saucer. I did as I was told and started shooting my own pix of the saucer and of Dave shooting pix and the land yacht all in the same frame.

After a few minutes of photography Dave walked across the brushy space between the road and the saucer, then stood there beside it with his hands on his hips, glaring at it. At last he reached out and touched it, gingerly at first as though it might be hot or might give him a static electricity shock, but then he took the flat of his hand and smacked the smooth metallic surface hard. If it had been a bell it would have rung from the slap, but as it was the sound was more like a thud as if he had smacked his hand into concrete. He waited a moment and then did it again with the same result.

"Maybe there's a door bell." I said, taking another pic of him standing beside the saucer.

"If there is I don't see it," he said, stepping back. He looked from the saucer to the ground around it and spotted a fair-sized rock. He walked over and picked it up. It was a handful and looked like pink granite. He went back to where he was beside the saucer, drew back his arm and began pounding on the metallic side. He hit it a half dozen times before stopping to check if he had done any damage. He hadn't. The gleaming side looked as though it had just been polished without as much as a finger smudge on it. After a little, Dave set at pounding on the side of the ship again with what seemed a little more ire, but with the same result.

"I don't think there's anybody home, Dave."

"Bastards!" he said, and took to pounding on the side of the ship like a mad man.

I let him go at it for a little while but it was hot and I knew he couldn't keep at it long, so when he began to slow down I stepped up and grabbed his wrist as he took another swing. "Forget it, Dave. They ain't home or they ain't coming to the door, so forget it." He was dripping with sweat and breathing pretty hard. He'd really been laying into his shots. "Come on back to the car and let's get some water and some air conditioning," I said. I took the rock from him and dropped it on the ground, then put my arm around his shoulders and led him back to the car.

We got in and started up the Lincoln to get the AC blowing and I got a couple of bottles of water out of the fridge in the rear. Turns out there were a couple of cans of Fosters lager in there too so I got them out as well.

Dave drank his bottle of water and I drank mine, then we popped the beers and took a sip. After a bit I asked, "You OK now?"

"Yeah, I suppose. Pisses me off though. Bastards kidnap us and stick things up my ass and then leave us to the cops like we were a couple of tagged coyotes without as much as a by-your-leave or a kiss-my-rosy-ass, and now they won't even come out to apologize for all the trouble they caused us."

"Yeah, it is ... perplexing."

"*Perplexing*," Dave snorted. "I'd say *perplexing*, just don't quite cover it. Why for a plug nickel I'd turn this damn Lincoln around and ram it right into that thing! Perplexing!"

They must have had some way of listening to what was going on in the Lincoln or maybe it was just coincidence, but Dave had no more than drawn another breath before there was a whirring sound that drew our attention back to the saucer and we saw a ramp coming down like a draw bridge from the side, a little to the right of where Dave had been pounding with his rock.

Dave was out of the car and running toward the spaceship before I could hardly take it in, but when it did get through my neurons what he was doing I rolled out and tried to catch him.

The ramp hit the ground about the time Dave got to the saucer and he had taken a couple of steps up toward the opening when the same two guys we had picked up hitchhiking stepped out and started down. They weren't dressed as Airmen now. They were in jeans and t-shirts. Dave didn't even slow down. He opened his arms like a man about to make a tackle and hit both of the Airmen like a runaway truck. They all went down in a heap and after a moment Dave sorted it out enough that he was sitting on one guy's chest and holding the other one by the collar, shaking him like a terrier shaking a rat.

Just as my foot hit the bottom of the ramp a swarm of little gray guys with big heads and black bug eyes came pouring out of the door and covered Dave like ants swarming over a sugar cube. I wasn't exactly sure what to do, but when I reached the swarm I piled in with both fists and both feet. Don't know that I did much good because there were a mess of 'em and the two humans had managed to get loose and start fighting back, but I gave it all I had until something hit me like a lightning bolt and I lost consciousness.

I came to back in the cell where I had spent the previous night, or one just like it. I was alone and felt like I had been worked over with a rubber hose, but I had some mad left from the fight so when I managed to get myself out of the bunk I went and grabbed hold of the bars and started screaming for the jailer. It didn't take long for an SP to show up.

"Hey, shut up in there," he ordered.

"Let me outta here! I didn't do anything. Where's Dave? What the hell are you people doing?"

"Your friend is OK," the cop said. "He just hasn't come out of the zap they hit him with. Said it took three shots to knock him out. That is one strong SOB."

The guy that had called himself Bob Jones came in and said, "Thank you, Airman. I'll take care of Mr. Helm now."

The cop said, "Yes sir," and didn't salute, though he looked like he wanted to before he turned and went out.

"Where's Dave?" I demanded.

Jones didn't come too close, like he was afraid I was gonna reach through the bars and throttle him, which I might have if he had tempted me a little more. He said, "It's just like the Airman told you. He is just waking up. He's a little groggy."

"How the hell did I get back here?"

"Mr. Smith and Mr. Black brought you back after the melee at the ship."

"Smith and Black?"

"The guys you picked up the other night."

"Friends of yours, are they?" I asked, beginning to put two and two together. "They work for Project Blue Book too?"

Jones didn't answer me, but he gave me a long speculative look. "Your friend is gonna be fine in a couple of hours and we'll have a little confab then—try to figure out what we are gonna do with you two," he said, shaking his head. He turned away, leaving me looking through the bars. I stared at the doorway he went out of for a while, then I went and sat down on the bunk again, thinking that I was truly in deep shit this time. An agent of the US government had just told be they were figuring out what to do with me so visions of lonely desert graves began to creep into my head, and then a vision of a small cell on a tropical island pushed that one out and I really started worrying. Nobody but Dave and my captors knew where I was. They could make me disappear like a fart in a hurricane and no one would be the wiser. That was when I started praying. "Oh Lord, if you get me out of this I won't ever do another stupid thing in my life."

But I could only plead with God for so long before the other part of my mind began ticking over. Had Dave and I really been in a fight with little gray flying saucer men, or had my cheese just slid off my cracker?

The promised two hours passed and then a couple more passed. I noticed that my Timex watch was stopped at 2:00. So much for "takes a licking..." Two M16-toting Airmen came in followed by Brother Jones. He held up a set of handcuffs, dangling them from an index finger. "You gonna be nice or do we need these?" he asked.

I took a deep breath and said, "I'll be nice," but I privately thought ... *all depends on how things go.*

He unlocked the cell and the Airmen fell in on either side of me and we marched out with Jones in front. It occurred to me that I could throw a choke hold on Jones and have him down on the floor before the guards could actually do anything, but I let the thought go. It wouldn't accomplish anything except maybe get me killed.

In the room where we had eaten breakfast the day before Dave was sitting at the table with a cup of coffee in front of him. He looked a little the worse for wear. When we marched in he popped to his feet with a, "You OK, G?"

"I'm alright. How about you? They said they had to hit you three times with that taser thing."

He grinned, looking more wolfish than sheepish as he sat back down. I took the chair across the table from him and a cup of coffee appeared in front of me which smelled wonderful. I picked it up and took a sip.

Jones sat down and the guards left the room. He looked from Dave to me and then back.

"What we oughta do is take you two idiots out in the desert and just shoot ya. It would make my life a hell of a lot easier. Why the hell didn't ya just go home?"

"If you and your little gray buddies had just let us be we'd probably have done just that," Dave began. "But nobody sticks nothin' up my ass without my permission. It just ain't acceptable. I don't give a damn if they *are* from Alpha Centauri or wherever."

"You went looking for trouble!" Jones snapped.

"They started it," I said.

He held up his hands in, if not surrender then at least in acknowledgement.

An Airman came in carrying a stack of papers which he placed in front of Jones. He placed two ballpoints above the stack then went out.

"OK," Jones began. "What we gonna do is have you two sign some papers swearing you won't tell anyone anything about what has been going on here and then you are gonna get in your car and go away."

"I am signing nothing until I get some more information," Dave said.

"Me too," I added.

Jones looked from one to the other of us with a disgusted look on his face. "Are you guys crazy? This is all top secret, and under the Homeland safety laws I could legally just pack you off to Guantanamo or some lesser-known and not nearly as nice a place. I'm trying to do this without completely violating your constitutional rights."

"Seems to me like the Constitution got flushed a long time ago. When you let these little bastards trap innocent travelers for their experiments that pretty well violated my rights," Dave said.

"Yeah, why did you let 'em do that, Bob?" I chimed in.

Jones seemed a little abashed and finally said, "I told 'em I didn't think it was a good idea, but the powers that be give these guys a pretty good bit of latitude. We owe them a lot—and frankly, we're more than a little afraid of 'em. When they showed up in New Mexico back in '48 they made it clear they would and could make us hurt pretty bad if we didn't give back the pilot from that crash near Roswell."

"I thought that crash and stuff was all just urban legend," Dave said.

"So far as the rest of the world is concerned it is. There aren't too many people that know what really happened. Not even me, but I do know that after that the little gray guys began coming and going pretty freely and people began getting picked up here and there for whatever the grays wanted. They promised not to really hurt anyone but they have traumatized a lot of people over the years."

"So all the flying saucer reports are true?" I asked.

Jones shrugged. "Some are, some aren't. Some really are just mass hysteria or hoaxes, but some are for real."

"How about all the 'Ancient Astronauts' stuff," Dave asked.

"I don't know. I am just a low level gopher working with the ETLO trying to keep the lid on all this mess, which brings me back to these non-disclosure agreements. If you'll just sign 'em and abide by 'em we can be done with all this crap and you can go home."

"And if not?" I asked.

"I wasn't kidding about Guantanamo. No signatures, you guys are on a transport out of here this afternoon to I don't *even* want to think about where, so maybe you oughta consider this for a little while."

Needless to say, we signed. They took all the pix out of the cameras and erased the memories and made sure we understood that the threats they were making were not idle at all. On the way home Dave said, "Doesn't matter if we keep quiet or not anyway. They have done such a thorough job of discrediting all the UFO hunters and seers that we wouldn't be believed anyhow."

"Still, they are gonna be watching us all the same," I said. "So we better keep our mouths shut."

Dave shrugged. "I guess. But how are they gonna know if we do talk? You think they have agents in the Windy City?"

"I think that after they fluoroscoped us they didn't say if they found anything."

Dave's attention snapped to me. "You mean you think they really did tag us?"

"I'm saying that whether they did or not I ain't gonna take the chance and tell anyone about anything that happened in Nevada."

After a little, Dave said, "Yeah, I guess."

# Hidden

by *Peter Glassborow*

George never found out what freak effect Dion Reynolds thought he had accidentally discovered when he hid his truck. He hardly offered any explanation at all. He merely said he had found it, was using it, and unless somebody could show him it was definitely against one of the company's rules, as laid out in the employment agreement, he would damn well continue using it.

Much later, George desperately wished that he had pressured Dion into telling him what he thought. Because he must have had some opinion, some theory he had formed that was different from George's that might, in his moment of need, have given him hope. Dion was not completely stupid. Everyone thought of him as stupid, but there were odd things where Dion showed a fast, cunning thought pattern. George suspected it was more intuition. Like an animal just knows to avoid some things and go for others, Dion just instinctively knew things even if he didn't understand them.

Dion was normally stupid, though. For a truck driver he was well paid, yet still he risked losing his job by hiding somewhere for part of every day, doing nothing, then claiming a delivery had taken a long time. Even stupider, he hid out on the company's own site. There were a thousand different places where a truck driver could hide in East Auckland, places he could just park and put up his feet. Why on Earth find a place on the company's own site? Now, that screamed stupid.

George had to admit it, Dion had found the perfect place to park up and hide. He not only found it but kept it a secret until George tracked him down. George found him by luck more than anything. Dion not only found the spot but also knew how it worked, and how to camouflage it so nobody else used it.

It was Ronz who set George on the path to finding Dion's hiding place. Ronz was the company's transport manager. That put Dion under his control. The company had eighteen trucks and drivers for hauling things both short and long distance.

The drivers were typical working class men, and as far as George and the other security staff were concerned the drivers were little trouble. But there's always one like Dion.

Ronz arrived at the security office and George buzzed him in. "George, I need to see where one of my drivers is," he said as soon as he was through the door.

George knew he almost certainly meant Dion. It wasn't the first time Ronz had asked him to discover where one of his drivers was, or had been. He had asked several times this past year, and it usually meant Dion.

Ronz, or Ronald Ziefelde, to give him his full name, was a good transport manager who ran the drivers efficiently and sensibly. If someone wanted to make a short private diversion and drop off or pick up something using the company truck, that was okay with Ronz—just let him know what you were doing and make up the lost time by the end of the day. "Better I know what they're doing and when," Ronz would say. "They'll do it anyway if I say no. This way I can make allowances for it."

George was happy to help. At the end of the day it was his job as a security guard to prevent losses, whether they were actual thefts or workers claiming pay for hours they hadn't worked. It was due to the latter that everyone had to swipe their ID cards at the gates when they entered or left. There wasn't much loss of either type, so George counted each success for security as rather sweet.

George had worked for the company for eight long and weary years. There was only so much enthusiasm he could work up for monitoring CCTV, patrolling the grounds, locking and unlocking doors or making new photo ID cards. The occasional hunt for a dishonest person made the middle-aged George wake up and show a younger man's interest in life. An actual success at catching someone was the cherry on top of the ice cream. Plus, at the back of his mind George hoped doing the company a good service might get him noticed and spark an actual pay rise. He'd been at exactly the same pay grade since he'd started.

Dion wasn't the only one that Ronz checked up on from time to time. When a driver wasn't on the company site when they were supposed to be, or said they had been somewhere when Ronz was sure they hadn't, or had gone through one of the three road gates at a time they shouldn't, then Ronz checked up on them using the security computer and video tapes. The last three times he came to security, it was for Dion. This was the fourth time. George knew, because he went back through the logbook to make sure.

George always read the log anyway when he came on duty to see what was new. Even when he came back from his annual three weeks holiday George always slogged through the previous three weeks' log entries so he knew what had been happening. Everything the security officers did they were supposed to log, and helping Ronz to check on Dion was something they had to log in case someone claimed a violation of the privacy laws, or some such rubbish.

John, the other guard George was on shift with, was off on a mobile foot patrol. That's what they called it, but actually it meant wandering around the site for an hour rather than sitting in the office. It was George's turn to sit in the office. That meant monitoring all the CCTV cameras and seeing to the odd visitor needing a replacement ID card or to sign out a key. At least Ronz had brought him something interesting to do.

"It's Dion again," Ronz told him.

"What's he done this time?"

"Hiding on site when he should be doing another run." Ronz explained that Dion was on local runs this week, going round Auckland picking up and dropping off lots of small packages and items. Dion was supposed to be available all day for this but had not reported back from the last run yet. The radio was out on Dion's truck so Ronz couldn't call him and he had assumed that Dion was still out. Then one of the other drivers told Ronz he had seen Dion come on site.

"What time?"

"About two-fifteen."

"Know what gate?"

"Not sure. Springs Road, probably."

George checked the computer for a report on Dion's card to see if it had been used that afternoon. Staff were supposed to swipe their cards to enter or leave. Visitors talked to security over the intercom and said who they were and where they were going. The security officer then pushed the appropriate button and the gate slid open.

The computer report said Dion's card had not been used that day, but George knew people like Dion were liable to follow somebody else in or out so that it wasn't recorded. There were always staff members sneaking out early, or in late, using that method.

With nothing on the computer the next thing was to try and spot Dion on the videotapes. There were three gates: Kerwyn, Springs and Allens Road. Allens was mostly for the staff, the other two were for goods vehicles and visitors. Kerwyn got the greatest use, as it was the one closest to inwards goods and the entrance to the main factory. Springs and Allens had cameras up on buildings watching them. Kerwyn was covered by a PTZ camera—that is, Pan-Tilt-Zoom.

There were twenty-three cameras altogether. Fixed ones, like on Springs and Allens, were set to cover entrances to buildings, inside inwards goods and dispatch. The rest were all PTZ and covered the outside of buildings. They used standard videotapes to film everything with twelve hours from six cameras on each tape.

As it was just after 4pm, what Ronz needed would be on the current tape. As George pressed the rewind button for Springs gate he asked, "He's not on site?"

Ronz shook his head. "I drove around the site. Can't see his truck anywhere." George had noticed Ronz's big, red American classic car cruising around thirty minutes earlier, popping up on one camera after another. "If he's hiding the truck he's doing it well."

The site was big and sprawling with old buildings mixed up with the new, and lately a lot of newly planted trees and extensive flowerbeds had been added. But it was hardly easy to hide a truck, and Ronz knew all the service roads and odd corners. If he couldn't find Dion then it seemed obvious to George that Dion wasn't here. He didn't say that to Ronz. George's theory was that Dion simply left the site to avoid work, his leaving and re-entering being done behind someone else so that it wasn't recorded on the computer. To catch Dion red-handed George had to catch these movements on the video. Good detective work like that should gain him some recognition at least.

They started looking at the Springs gate video from 2pm. George had it on fast forward, as a big blue truck would stand out even at the fastest speed. They watched from two until two-thirty as superfast vehicles and pedestrians came and went through the gate. They saw nothing like Dion's truck.

Next they looked at the replay of the camera covering Allens with similar results. The Kerwyn camera was different though as it was a constantly rotating PTZ model. It was harder to keep attention as the camera was revolving through 360 degrees and watching the video could make your eyes go funny even at normal speed. George had to keep stopping when either of them thought they had seen something.

They'd almost given up hope when there was a brief blur of blue at the edge of the screen. Rewinding and playing at normal speed there was the glimpse of a blue truck coming in behind a car.

"That him?" George asked.

Ronz frowned. "Not sure. Can you replay it?"

The replay was of little help. There were so many different trucks and vans coming in and out in so many different colours that it was impossible to say it was even one of the company's trucks, let alone the one that Dion drove. Having the PTZ's moving video image was not always an advantage.

Ronz decided that he couldn't say for sure that it was Dion's truck, and left.

But there was something on another of the PTZ cameras, number 4. As it panned round it covered a door that led from the service road into the IT office. There was one frame where someone must have just opened the door and it caught a reflection of something blue in the door's glass. After George had looked at the video several times and was sure what he was seeing he waited until it was time to change round with John.

George walked around to the door that had held the reflection. He had formed the theory that because the door was at an angle when it opened it showed a truck just parked, or passing by, a triangle of waste ground. This waste ground was in an angle formed by two buildings. The Information Technology building was on the left, and the electrical building on the right. The electrical building held various switchboards to distribute power around the site, plus it housed the emergency generator. The two ends of the buildings almost touched, forming the apex of the triangle and the service road the third side.

Looking around, George was sure this area had been checked out by Ronz. And if the truck had been passing the spot it would have shown up on other PTZs a few seconds later. So it was a mystery.

George decided to put the whole thing to the back of his mind until the following week. The security office was having a big upgrade with a new hardware and software package that replaced the old swipe cards with a proximity model. All the VCRs were to be replaced, with all video to be stored on hard drives for ten days. Now reviewing videos would be much easier, as finding a particular time and date would be simpler. They could also play the videos super slow or even faster than before. They could even take one quarter of a video and enlarge it to fill the whole screen. After the installation was completed George hoped to find the answer to Dion's absences.

A few days after the installation George came in for the afternoon shift and saw in the log that Ronz had requested a check of the ID card records for that day and a viewing of some of the videos as well. It was Dion again. The log said they had found nothing conclusive. That was when George remembered about the IT door's reflection. Dion's disappearances still kept bothering him, as if it were a competition between the two of them. Dion obviously had some great way of hiding his truck on the site, and George wanted desperately to find out where it was, and hopefully gain praise for his work.

George noted the times that the search had been conducted and spent the rest of the evening, when he was in the office, going through the camera 4 video slowly. Eventually George found the blue reflection again.

Ronz had suspected that Dion hadn't left the site until nearly 08:15, when he should have been loaded and gone long before 08:00. The log said they had caught a glimpse of a blue truck leaving the site through the Kerwyn gate at 08:29. What George eventually found was that at 08:22 somebody had stood in the IT door entrance talking with another. The person in the entrance was holding the door open at an angle, and reflected in the glass there was a definite blue flash. George went through the video of the nearest camera to the scrap of waste ground, and there was one of the company's trucks coming along the narrow service road that ran alongside it at 08:28. This service road headed right towards the Kerwyn gate.

What he couldn't figure out was where Dion had been concealing the truck in the meantime. Rewinding further, George saw Dion leaving the loading bay at 07:36, heading towards the scrap of ground at 07:37. Apart from the blue flash at 08:27 there was nothing until he left through the gate at 08:29.

When it was George's turn to go on foot patrol he walked to the waste ground. Its triangular shape was big enough to hold a truck but there was no way to conceal anything from anyone using the road. Apart from the ends of the two buildings there were just some weeds, odds and ends of rubbish and a rusting triangle of corrugated iron leaning against the wall of the IT building.

George stood on the kerb, wondering what it all meant. He looked down and saw scuffmarks on the kerb. They were clearly made by a vehicle driving up and across the kerb onto the waste ground, and judging by their size they were from a truck. There was no reason for anyone to drive up here so it had to be Dion's truck. The tire marks continued for a few metres onto the waste ground then stopped. If Dion had parked there the end of the truck would only be centimetres from the road. Clearly it could not be hidden like that. Even if Dion had driven all the way onto the waste ground there were only two more metres to go before the truck would have been hard up against the two walls where they nearly joined together at the apex. Here there was a one and a half metre space between the buildings that had been blocked off with a wooden fence. George gave it a good kick. It was definitely solid.

Whatever Dion had done with his truck was beyond him. Looking at it logically, any other person would say that Dion obviously hadn't hidden his truck and himself here, that it was just a string of circumstances. That wasn't how George saw it now. There was something about that waste ground and the flash of blue reflection on the video that ate away at him. Maybe it was just that he had such a boring job and it gave George a chance to exercise his intelligence, but he couldn't let it go. He *would* outwit Dion.

The following week George was back on the morning shift. He was in the security office when Ronz called on the phone. He had lost contact on the radio with Dion and suspected he was hiding out again. Could security try and locate him on camera?

George immediately viewed camera 4, hoping for evidence of a blue flash reflected in the door—but no luck. When Roger, his partner for that shift, arrived to swap jobs, George left him to look at the rest of the videos while he went for a foot patrol.

It was 08:12 when George reached the waste ground. There was no sign of Dion or his truck; just weeds, rubbish and the piece of corrugated iron resting against the wooden fence at the buildings' apex. George continued along the service road. There was a corner fifty metres ahead. He was just walking round it when Roger called him on the radio. There was a problem with an automatic door in one of the buildings and could George go check it out? As George turned round to head towards the faulty door, a company truck reversed off the waste ground. The truck bumped out onto the road, then reversed direction and swung towards him. George stepped off the road to let it past. Dion was driving.

George stood stunned. This was impossible. He had just walked past the waste ground and there had been nothing there, and he would have heard if it had come up the road behind him. Dion must have somehow hidden the truck right under his nose.

As the truck passed, Dion looked down and gave George one of his sneers. It was the sort that made him think Dion saw him as some middle-aged, pot-bellied has-been, and he wanted to just reach up and smack Dion across the face. The truck swung around the corner and away from him in a puff of diesel exhaust fumes.

George walked onto the waste ground and looked around. There were the weeds, rubbish and the corrugated iron against the IT wall. There were the tire marks where the truck had parked on the waste ground then reversed back out. There was nothing to indicate how Dion had hidden the truck. And George knew he had hidden the truck, hidden it well because less than a minute before George had walked past that very spot and there had been no truck there.

George looked around again. Even the finest camouflage artist couldn't have hidden a four-wheeled diesel-engine truck on that waste ground. He walked around, looking for something to indicate how Dion had done it. Roger called him on the radio again but he ignored him. He had to think.

He didn't know what he was looking for. Maybe some sort of trap door in the ground—except that was ridiculous. How could there be such a thing? And there were no doors in the walls of the two buildings that could be used even by just a driver on foot.

George tried to remember what had happened, going back over it in his mind. He had walked past the waste ground. There was nothing there. Tire tracks, corrugated iron scrap, weeds, rubbish. Nothing else. George had continued along the service road almost to the corner, and then Roger had called on the radio about the faulty door. As George talked to him there had been the rumbling of a truck engine in the background.

That was it!

There had been the rumble of a diesel engine while he was listening to Roger. The engine had been idling, not moving. Now George began walking back to the office, thinking furiously: as he had turned to retrace his steps after Roger's call the engine's note increased. That was because the truck had rolled out onto the service road. The corner of the electrical building hid the full view of waste ground when George was at the corner so he couldn't see where Dion had started from. Though, of course, George knew where he had been because of the tire marks in the clay and weeds.

Then, as George had turned to retrace his steps and fix the faulty door the engine revved, the truck rolled out across the kerb, and Dion gave him his sneer.

Why had the engine been idling? George walked slowly back to the office to see what Roger wanted. He would say he had to come back as the radio was faulty and only receiving. That would give him an excuse to walk slowly and think fast.

He was nearly at the office door when a thought struck him. When he had first gone past the waste ground the triangle of corrugated iron was leaning against the wooden fence. When George walked past the ground the second time, after Dion had driven off, the corrugated iron was back against the IT wall.

When George heard the truck's engine idling, had Dion been out of the cab, placing the iron back against the IT wall? Was that what he was doing? And if so, why? What could a piece of old iron do?

Later on when he had time George carefully checked all the cameras. There was Dion driving towards the service road at 07:41, and away at 08:14. But nothing showed him approaching it at the time George had been there. That meant he had been at the waste ground since just after 07:41.

And there he'd hidden the truck somehow.

Before he went home that evening George walked around the waste ground with a torch, the big one from the office. He looked at the corrugated iron, thinking it might be the trigger for something to happen, perhaps tied to a switch or tripwire or something. He moved it cautiously a few centimetres to see if something happened. The hairs on the back of his neck tingled in anticipation of revealing Dion's trick. But then nothing happened, so he put it back. George walked away confused.

It was a day later that George thought of using his car as a trigger, because maybe it required a heavy object to trigger whatever Dion had rigged up to hide the truck. Because that's what must be happening, George decided. Dion had something concealed that sprung up, or over, and hid the truck. He would keep searching, and could try his own car if nothing else worked.

George looked everywhere for whatever it was that Dion was using, everywhere except inside the two buildings that formed the triangle. Those George inspected on the next Sunday at 06:30 when they were empty.

There was nothing in either of them. In the electrical building there were signs warning of high voltage and only authorised staff to enter. There was the humming of the switchboards. There was no camouflage net here. Some lengths of old electrical cable and a lot of dust on the floor. Nothing else.

The IT area was an annex extending from the main administration building. There were several rows of desks and computers. A separate room held the mainframe. Signs warned only authorised staff to enter. Several cupboards were full of switchboards, cables and odds and ends that had been replaced. There was no sign of any sort of camouflage device in there either.

George used a ladder to look on both roofs, but there was nothing out of the ordinary. That day he was on duty with Mike, who asked George what he was doing. Mike said he'd caught sight of George on a roof on one of the cameras. George told him that he suspected there was a blocked drain as there had been a minor leak in the last downpour. It was a pathetic story, but as it was Sunday morning Mike was more interested in reading the papers than doing much of an investigation into George's activities or motives.

George was in the office from eight until nine. It was the typical Sunday morning: a few maintenance staff working on the production lines, a few office staff catching up.

At nine Mike and George swapped around again. George grabbed his car keys and went straight out to the car park. His car was a small Honda, so he was careful driving onto the waste ground in case it bottomed on the weeds and the odd bit of rubbish. Holding his breath, he stopped where the truck tire tracks ended. Nothing happened and George was disappointed.

He could see the corrugated iron lying against the IT wall. Before, George had suspected that Dion was moving the piece of iron around as some sort of trigger. George had discarded that theory, as the iron wasn't attached to anything. Deciding he would check it again he got out of the car and walked across to the scrap of iron. It was less than a metre in length on its longest axis and painted a green that had faded with the sun and rain with rust eating its way into the iron in many places. He picked it up to see if there was the slightest possibility that something had been attached to it.

As George lifted the iron something weird happened. The hairs on the back of his neck stood up. George could feel them stir, and looking at his forearms the hairs there were all straight up as well. It was most peculiar.

Looking round, nothing looked different and George put the iron down where it had been. He slowly walked back to his car. As he did, the hairs on his body all settled down again. Now George noticed that something felt odd about the two-metre strip of ground between his car and the iron. Had he felt it before when he had examined this ground on foot? George wasn't sure.

George found it impossible to pin down what he felt. Something felt different; like the tingle that runs through your shoulders when you think someone's watching you. He looked around warily. It wasn't the ground, which was just scuffed clay and weeds, or the walls of the building; it was the air around him. It felt alive, like the difference between tap water and a fizzy drink. The air was now fizzy and thick. It was barely perceptible but definitely there. When he stepped into the area he felt it. He couldn't have described it any better than that: thick, fizzy air.

He walked back to the iron and lifted it up. The hairs on his arms lifted again. Why hadn't he noticed this before? It was a very still day, so George thought maybe that's what allowed him to notice. Or maybe he was so desperate to find out Dion's mystery that he was more perceptive than before. Either way there was definitely an effervescence in the air around the car and lifting up the iron again made all his hair stand electrified.

George wanted to experiment some more. He recalled the moment just before Dion had driven out onto the road. George had walked past and the corrugated iron had been off against the wooden fence at the apex of the triangle. Now he tried to place it where he remembered it had been that time. This time when George walked back to the car the hairs on his body stayed up, and the air felt fizzier and heavier than before. Whatever was happening in this triangle, the piece of corrugated iron's location changed it, made it stronger. With the iron resting against the wall, there was but the slightest sensation in the air between the iron and the car. But when George moved the iron only slightly away from the IT wall it made his hair stand up. When he put the iron against the fence, the sensation hit him like a wave of vertigo.

George wondered what would happen if he moved the car closer to the wooden fence. Was that what Dion did with the truck? If he did then it was without leaving any tire tracks.

Back behind the steering wheel George could still feel the prickling in the air. His hairs were still upright and the air, even in the car, was positively fizzing. How had he never noticed this before?

He put the car in gear and crept forward.

George felt the tingling air wash over him like a thousand small beestings as the car crept forward. The stings seemed to intensify as he moved closer to the fence until it almost hurt. It felt like every hair on his body was standing so straight that they were now all fighting to pluck themselves from his skin. He thought his mind might be playing tricks on him. He moved forward until the front bumper was almost touching the wooden fence, but nothing else happened. He looked back. There were a few flattened weeds and the faint traces of his tire tracks. Dion's tire marks had not extended this far, so clearly he hadn't done this.

George replaced the corrugated iron back where it had been against the IT wall. The feeling shrank and his body hairs settled. Back in the car, George could still feel the strangeness of that area— subdued, but still there. Reversing onto the road, he drove back into the car park.

He was locking the car when the radio suddenly burst into life. "Can you hear me now?" came Mike's voice, a little annoyed.

"Yes."

"What happened?"

"When?"

"When you disappeared. What were you doing driving round the site?"

"Nothing. Just trying to figure out what the scraping noise is that I get from one wheel."

"Probably a stone in the brake drums. What happened to the radio?"

"Nothing. Why, were you calling me?"

"Hell of a screeching from it. Had to turn it off. Just turned it back on now when I saw you park up."

"No, nothing to do with me. Must be the base set."

It was when George was home that evening having dinner with his wife that he realised why nothing had happened. He was sitting at the kitchen table waiting while his wife dished up the meal accompanied by her usual listing of everything that had gone on with her day. Trying to blot out her moaning, George tried to visualise what Dion had done different from him when he drove onto the waste ground.

George had in his mind's eye a picture of his car overlaying Dion's truck, both driving across the kerb and stopping in the same spot. There was Dion and he leaving the engines running while they walked forward and moved the corrugated iron. Both felt a fizz in the air as they crossed the few metres to the wall. Both felt their hair stand on end as they moved the piece of corrugated iron away from the IT wall. Both walked back to their vehicles through the fizzy zone, which was now feeling even fizzier. Dion climbed up into the cab. George dropped down behind the wheel. Both put the vehicles into gear and eased off the clutches. The car and the truck, superimposed on each other in George's mind, crept forward through the zone of fizzy air. Something happened to Dion's truck but not to George's car. But what? Something that did not leave tire tracks for Dion. Or did he move the truck forward at all? Maybe he stayed in the same place and did something else. What was it?

After a mediocre dinner, and as he stacked the dishes in the dishwasher, George ran through it again. Driving across the kerb. Stopping in the same place. Walking through the fizzy air. Moving the corrugated iron. Hairs rising. Walking back through the fizzy air. Dion climbed up into his cab. George dropped down into his seat.

The obvious difference smacked George right in the intellect. The difference wasn't in what Dion and George had done. The difference was in the size of their vehicles. George's car; Dion's truck. If moving a piece of corrugated iron could bring this thing on then a bigger metallic object, like a truck, must have another effect on it. Unless the metallic object wasn't big enough, such as it only being a small Honda.

The following Saturday, George borrowed his brother's 4×4 SUV, leaving him the Honda. George's wife whined that he had a perfectly good Honda and why did he need a great big SUV? George told her the same thing he had told his brother, that he was helping someone move house and he needed to move something on a trailer for them.

George was on the afternoon shift, 3 till 11pm. He waited until it was dark, after nine, before rolling the big SUV round to the waste ground. There was nobody on the site except for George and the other guard, Sammi, who was safely set up in the office listening to some Pacific Island talk-back programme. George told Sammi he didn't mind staying out a little longer than normal if the radio programme was good.

George stopped on the waste ground where the tire marks ended. It had been raining and he could see the SUV would leave heavier tire marks in the clay, but that shouldn't matter, as it was only Dion and George who cared about this waste ground. Walking across the short distance to the corrugated iron he felt the slight tingling in the air. As soon as George moved the iron the hairs were there, underneath the raincoat he wore, bristling from his forearms up against the nylon, raising on the back of his neck and every other part of his body, as far as he could tell.

Leaning the iron against the wooden fence, he walked the few paces back to the SUV. The feeling around him was much stronger. George sat in the driver's seat for a few seconds, collecting his thoughts. Firstly, there was concern that when George triggered Dion's trick something might happen to his brother's two-year-old SUV. It would take him forever to pay for that if it were damaged. Secondly, he was concerned about what might happen to him. That was only a slight concern, as George had seen no harm come to Dion. Third, was what might happen if Dion realised that George had found out how his trick had worked. George suspected he might get real vicious when angry.

"No point thinking about it," George told himself. "Just do it." He made sure the seatbelt was done up, headlights on high beam, four wheel drive engaged, and let out the clutch. The first of the weeds, bleached white by the headlights' glare, disappeared under the front bumper. George hardly touched the accelerator, so the speed was the slowest he could manage. There were only two metres to go before he reached the fence. He dare not damage the SUV so. George was concentrating hard and sweating under the nylon coat.

He was stunned to see the view in front of him begin splitting. The end of the IT building was disappearing to the left while the electrical building went to the right. Neither wall was actually moving; it was like the ends of the buildings were being rolled inwards so that the apex of the triangle where the wooden fence had been was expanding. And the fence itself was gone. In its place was a darker patch of ground that extended well away from the SUV.

Although shocked by what was happening, part of George's mind was still monitoring his driving as the buildings continued to roll away. Realising that he must have travelled the two metres towards the wooden fence already George slowed down even more. Even so, within five seconds the rolling up had extended to either side so that George had to twist his head left and right to keep the ends in view. With a few seconds more the buildings had rolled up almost out of sight. All that was left was a dwindling strip of the company's site behind him that George could see in the rear view mirror. Then that was gone as well and he braked and put the vehicle in neutral.

All around him was now a dark landscape. In front, the SUV seemed to be on a small rocky outcrop with the ground a few metres out dropping away slightly so that he was looking across a shallow valley. The far side was about a kilometre away. Despite it being night he saw it wasn't really dark anymore, just dull, with the SUV's headlights only lighting things close. Looking left and right the landscape, he saw that the stretched away in gently rolling hills, adorned at the highest points with flat rocky outcroppings where the dirt had weathered away. Looking down from the driver's window, George could see that the ground seemed to be a mixture of coarse sand and small stones. The rocky outcrop the SUV was on was a kind of shale. It was all a dull reddy-brown.

Cautiously, George wound down the window and looked up. The sky was overcast, the clouds a mottled grey. The light was something similar to a late afternoon but very overcast as if there might be rain coming soon. The darkness of the ground made it seem darker than it was. "Now how the hell did you do this, Dion?" George asked himself. Then the smell of the outside air struck him fully as it replaced the air in the SUV. It was a sandy smell, definitely a smell that went along with the ground underneath.

Countries smell different. When George went to Fiji on a holiday, getting off the plane he could smell the foliage, that damp, rank jungle aroma. Europe smells different too, he had been told. And Mike, who had been in the merchant navy, had told George you could smell Africa from across the horizon. He said it was a dusty, spicy smell made up of all the plants and winds in Africa. This place smelled different from anywhere George had been before, like a vast desert. Or something close to being a desert as he could imagine, as George had never actually been in a one. He turned out the lights but left the engine running, making sure the handbrake was on tight before getting out of the SUV. The temperature was mild, slightly warmer than when he had got in the SUV at the car park. The ground was crunchy underfoot. He walked forward a pace or two to the edge of the rocky outcrop. The slope down into the valley wasn't steep, certainly something the SUV could handle, not that George was planning to drive down there. He picked up a round stone and threw it down slope. It bounced once before rolling a few metres further.

George checked behind the SUV. There were his tire marks going back about a metre and a half, and then nothing. His tire marks overlaid other faint marks, which George assumed were from Dion's truck. George noted that there was that odd effervescent feeling in the air here, the same as there was back on the waste ground.

He walked back towards where the kerb of the service road should be. There was nothing there, just more of the stones and sand. He walked far enough that it should have taken him well out onto the service road. There was still nothing there at all to show where the road had been, but the fizzy air feeling was gone.

George knew this was all impossible. He looked at his watch. Only a few minutes had elapsed since he had driven onto the waste ground.

He felt increasingly uncomfortable, his head swivelling on his shoulders uneasily, and he walked quickly back to the SUV. As George reached the tire tracks the weird, fizzy air feeling came back.

Once inside the car he took a quick look round at the deserted landscape. George debated turning the vehicle round but was too nervous to try anything different, so put the SUV into reverse and touched the accelerator with his foot.

George kept an eye on the rear view mirror. As soon as the SUV started to move the dark landscape began disappearing, reversing what had happened before. The dark landscape rolled up from the rear around both sides to the front. Replacing it was the familiarity of the company site. The glow from buildings and streetlights replaced the dark landscape. The familiar view continued rolling round to his front until the IT and electrical building unrolled from the flanks into the centre. George braked and hit the headlights and there was the apex of the triangle of waste ground with the wooden fence brightly lit up by the headlights as if it had never disappeared.

George's mind was in turmoil and he could not accept what had just happened. By no stretch of the imagination had that been some trick camouflage net, or trapdoor, or anything like that. It was like George was in another country. He reversed onto the road before he remembered the piece of corrugated iron. As soon as George put it back in its usual position against the IT wall the hairs went down on his body and the fizzy air feeling was reduced.

Back in the car park, something occurred to him. George bent down by the rear wheel and dug into the tread with the tip of his ballpoint pen. A small glob of sand and grit came out. George rubbed it between his fingers. This was physical proof of what had happened—it was not his imagination.

But what *had* happened?

The sand showed George had been in a real place. Where would there be a large, desolate, arid area like that? North Africa? Australia? The Gobi desert? Somewhere like that. How could he possibly go there and then back here so quickly?

The rest of the shift and for the next two days, George thought of nothing else and he soon realised he had to go back and look again. His memory of the fear he felt at the time was replaced by a desire to see it all again, and try and get some explanation. George had to find out what on Earth he had activated when driving his brother's SUV onto that triangular patch of waste ground. Was it a magnetic field or something similar—was that why the hairs on his body stood up? And the piece of corrugated iron, why did that reduce it when it was placed against the IT wall? Perhaps it distorted the field. And what did the modified field only do with a vehicle above a certain size?

George speculated it was something to do with the proximity of the electrical building and of the IT area. It was something to do with their locations on either side of the triangle. There was a lot of electricity involved with the electrical building. Perhaps somehow the IT area and its mainframe computers were doing something.

Had he been to another place on Earth? It had to be, because thinking about the alternative caused his pulse to quicken. He'd been able to breathe the air, he assured himself, and the gravity there had the same pull as on Earth. It had to be.

Moving to somewhere else on Earth was an idea George began to favour over anything else. Another place, an arid area of Earth. What a thing that would be if it were true. A way of moving to somewhere else on Earth with just an electrical building, an IT area and a service road forming a triangle.

He wondered how the hell Dion had found this place. And how had he found out how to switch it on and off with a piece of corrugated iron?

Going back again to the desert would be difficult, as George couldn't just use his brother's SUV any time. His brother had reluctantly agreed to let him use it to pull a trailer, but he was not the sort to keep letting George do that. He had the money in the family and he was not one for sharing. Nor would he believe the truth, not that George was ready to share it yet, and when he did he wanted any profit or praise to come to him. So George bought an SUV of his own.

He traded the Honda in for it, telling his wife the Honda was getting well past it. The HP payments would be difficult on his pay so his wife wasn't happy with that at all. Like him, she was on a low wage and often asked how they would get on when they had to retire as they had few savings.

George's SUV was considerably older than his brother's one, but slightly bigger dimensions and weight because George wanted to make sure it was big enough to trigger the triangle. However, before he tried again George wanted to talk to Dion.

George found Dion alone in the cafeteria one lunchtime. He walked up and sat down alongside Dion. George was blunt. "How did you find out about that place, Dion?"

"What place?"

"The desert. You drive onto that waste ground by the electrical building and into a desert. I've been there."

The expression on Dion's face slowly changed. An air of injured innocence was replaced by one of his sneers. "I found it," he replied. "I'm using it, and unless somebody can show me it was definitely against one of the company's rules I'll damn well continue using it."

"But do you know what you're doing?"

"None of your business, security man. So mind your own business and keep out of mine." That was the only conversation George had with Dion about the triangle of waste ground.

Easter was two weeks later. A long weekend on the evening shifts meant penal rates so George always worked them. Except this time it meant plenty of time to go exploring again. In those two weeks Dion had been given a second written warning by Ronz, so was being good and always sticking to his runs. There was virtually no chance that George would encounter him trying to use the triangle over Easter. A check on the computer would show if he had ever come on site outside of his normal hours, but he had never done that. Also his car was an ordinary size so not something he could trigger the triangle with. As the truck keys were all locked away in Ronz's desk draw after hours George was sure as he could be that Dion was out of the picture for Easter.

George had swapped shifts around with others so he was on every evening throughout the weekend. That meant four nights to use the triangle of waste ground. And it being Easter there was virtually no chance of anyone else being on site apart from a few maintenance staff, and the odd loser who had nothing else to do over the holiday.

George was tempted to try on the Thursday, but there was still an evening shift working in the factory making plastic components. It was Friday, after it had got dark, that George was ready to roll again.

This time he was going to take a little digital camera and his cell phone. George was going to try and ring the security office from the "other country". He knew the radio would be hopelessly out of range, and his phone was not configured for international calls, but he was going to try anyway.

With the camera George was going to put photos of the desert on his computer. George intended to examine them carefully. He hoped that he might detect something on them, something on the skyline, like a building or landmark, that would help him identify the area of the Earth he was on. George hadn't seen anything the first time, but then he was so stunned by everything that first time that it was quite possible he had overlooked the obvious.

Running everything through his mind George realised that he should take something with him to be able to see further while in the desert. A neighbour leant him a small pair of binoculars for that.

Of course he could just drive around in the SUV but George was terrified that once out of the fizzy air area he'd never get back. So his plan was to stop, look around and take pictures, and that was all.

At the last moment George grabbed the big torch from the office. It had been day in the desert while dark here, which he reasoned meant the desert was in a different time zone. But he would hate to find he needed a torch and didn't have one.

There was also the worry that he could end up somewhere completely different this time. George had a brief vision of the SUV rolling out into rush hour in Paris and getting arrested by a gendarme. He realised that wasn't logical. It would be the arid area again, George was sure of that. Well, fairly sure—after all Dion seemed to always go to the same place.

He waited until it was dark and it was his turn to go on foot patrol for an hour. George stopped the SUV at the kerb by the waste ground. He wanted to ensure everything was the same. In truth, George was shaking with fear now that the moment was here. Whatever was happening was outside most people's experience. He thought it probable this was something so unique that nobody else had ever experienced it before. Except for Dion, of course.

George had considered telling the police or someone about what had been found. But how would he explain it? "Hey, Officer, get in my car. I want to take you for a drive to a desert somewhere on the other side of the planet." George supposed he could do that, except he wanted the glory of this for himself. That was what George really wanted, to be the one who discovered the way of transporting yourself from one side of the planet to another.

George could see himself being famous. Being in all the papers. Getting rich, obviously, because someone would have to acknowledge what he had done, and there must be money in that. Of course there was Dion to contend with. George had thought of that as well. When George announced what he had discovered he wouldn't mention Dion at all. If Dion opened his mouth, George would say that Dion had copied him and was just trying to get in on the bandwagon.

He had his story all worked out. George would tell them he had worked out for himself that the triangle was a weird place because he had felt the strange fizzy air. George had speculated that it was some strange magnetic field. When he tried to drive his SUV onto it to see if it was affected George had found himself in the desert. Then, of course, there had been the discovery of that a scrap of metal, like a piece of corrugated iron, could switch the field off so that it couldn't transport anyone.

Scientists would be called in to investigate the field, and they would work out exactly what it was. Maybe it wasn't magnetic at all. Whatever it was they'd soon work it out, George was sure. Ways would be found to harness the field and then it would be a worldwide transport system. And all credit, and some money, should come his way and get him out of this miserable cycle of life. Brilliant!

Of course, George would decline the suggestion to have the field be named after him. That would be egotistical. George would not decline any money. That was sensible. And there had to be plenty of that, surely. Even if it was as a guest appearance on a TV talk show.

That was all in the future. Now for his second trip. George had wasted enough time looking round the triangle. It was all the same as before. The area with the fizzy air was in the same place. The corrugated iron was in the same place. When George moved it across to the wooden fence the hairs were up on his skin as usual.

Walking back to the SUV, the feeling in the triangle was stronger, now that the corrugated iron had been moved. Seat belt done up, George released the handbrake, put her in gear and rolled forward. This time George had the lights on dip and the twin beams wobbled on the fence as the SUV rolled across the uneven surface.

As George reached the last two metres before the wall, the wooden fence at the apex of the triangle disappeared and as before the two walls rolled up. This time George was ready for it, and he saw clearly what was happening. The two walls were not rolling up. Instead the view of the desert was spreading out from the centre, the desert view replacing the view of the buildings' walls. George eased the car along slowly and looked left and right as the desert replaced the company site. The last sliver of normality disappeared as he watched in the rear view mirror. The desert was all around him.

As before, George was on the rocky outcrop overlooking the shallow valley. The far side was a kilometre away. Everything seemed to be the same as before, except for the light. It was different; slightly pinker. George looked up. The clouds were the same grey, but there was a pinker tinge off to one side on the horizon where the sun must have been.

George turned off the lights and the engine. The SUV was old but reliable, so George was sure it would start again and not leave him stranded in the desert. Stepping out of the SUV, George was immediately struck by how much colder it was than before. Now the ground crunched underfoot. Putting a hand down, he knew why—it was freezing. Either there had just been a frost or it was getting ready for one.

All this seemed very odd. Before in the desert it had been a different time of the day, and even a different season from what it was now. It had only been a few weeks, hardly enough time for a big seasonal change. Maybe it was different in this desert, but the time of day in the desert should have been the same, because it was nearly the same time in the evening as the first journey.

George shivered—out of cold rather than fear. He was in shirtsleeves. He'd intended spending most of his hour here—though what he thought he would be doing apart from taking pictures he wasn't sure—but the cold gave him the impetus to get moving. First, George planned to take a 360-degree montage of the full horizon that could be examined later. Finding a clue to his location would help when George announced his discovery. He'd be able to say that he had found a way of going from latitude and longitude such and such, to latitude and longitude this and that. That made it sound a bit more scientific than that you needed a SUV above a certain weight to make it work, and a piece of rusting corrugated iron to switch it off.

He was going to shoot from the north then go east in a circle. Being a digital camera, George could take dozens of photos so that he should be able to get everything. He pulled out a small button compass to determine north, except it seemed a little reluctant to point anywhere. The needle just sat facing the same point on the compass's side no matter which way he turned the case. George wondered if the waste ground's field had affected it. He tapped it a bit and it finally twitched off to point almost directly across the valley. That seemed handy as that meant the valley ran roughly east-west. The pinker tinge in the sky was roughly northeast so he supposed it was the rising sun.

He picked out a rocky outcrop somewhere on the horizon that was roughly north and lined up the camera. He took the photo and looked down into the display to see if it had come out all right. It had, though it was a little dark, which George assumed was a result of the dark ground. He continued taking photos, moving right, making sure they overlapped. He clicked away, checking every third or fourth photo that it was still coming out all right.

George was almost back facing north again when he noticed a slight movement on the far side of the valley. It was a glimpse, like something had just passed a gap between rocks, making it visible for a second or two. Whether a vehicle, animal or human he couldn't tell.

George put the camera down on the bonnet and got the binoculars out of the SUV. He saw it again, briefly—a quick blur of shadow. He wasn't sure, but got the impression that it was moving from left to right. The binoculars were a small, low-magnification model. George had no idea how fast the object was been moving.

He saw movement again, definitely left to right this time. It seemed to be moving behind a line of rocks. Finally it came closer, emerging from the rocks and darting through a smaller cluster further down the valley. It stood on two legs and, George was certain, had the form of a human. The figure was wearing dark brown clothing and walking at the speed of a run.

The man—as George assumed it to be—came into the open. George tried to determine what he could at that distance. He formed the opinion that the man had on tight clothing, something like a jumpsuit as it clung to the skin. The man was in profile to George but seemed to be carrying something in his left hand, the hand on the far side—something like a walking stick, or perhaps a spear.

If George could talk to him, or try and talk, maybe he could find out where they were. George wanted to get some idea of their longitude and latitude. He got back in the SUV and flashed the lights and hit the horn a few times. George could see the distant figure, still travelling at his fast walk, continue for a few seconds, then stop and turn towards the SUV. The man seemed to crouch slightly and stare at it for several seconds. Then the man began running, straight towards George.

Whoever he was, shepherd or hunter, George could see he was fit. His long legs—he was exceptionally tall—carried him down the far side of the valley at an incredible sprint. He swerved around the larger rocks but cleared the others with long bounds. "Hell of a runner, mate," George complimented him as he got out of the SUV and picked up the binos again.

Viewing him closer through the binoculars, George was looking almost down on him now as he neared the valley bottom. He was so moving fast it was difficult to form an accurate picture of the man. As he hit the valley floor and began climbing towards the SUV George saw him much clearer now. What George saw sent a shiver right through him—this time, it was of fear.

The man was not wearing tight clothing; it was his skin. A dark brown, slightly glossy skin unhindered by even a scrap of cloth. No genitals were visible, so George was only assuming it was a male. Its head was hairless, and even from half a kilometre George could see dire intent in its stern face as its overlarge eyes glared fixedly up at him. He was tall. George was taller than average man, yet still he knew that this man would tower over him. Then George realised with a shocked gasp that the man was easily almost twice his height.

This was plainly not a man, not even a human at all, nor any ape or creature that man had ever known.

It had no hair at all, nor was there any fat on the creature's body—every inch was tough sinew and lean muscle. Its limbs were thin—no, not thin like a human, George told himself, but thinner-boned and larger-muscled. How could such bones support such mass of muscle? He knew instantly that this creature was far stronger than him, and its bones, he reasoned, far harder. From the glare of those eyes and the set of its face, now that he saw it closer, George thought he saw anger—or hunger.

George didn't know why that last thought entered his head, but it did. The very thought brought terror trembling to his lips, and he screamed. His body froze while his mind told him to climb back into the car. While he stood there, petrified, the dark brown creature whipped up the stick in its left hand. Now George saw it was bow and several arrows, held together in the left fist like a Mongol archer. The creature's right hand came forward, plucked out an arrow and fitted it to the bowstring all in one smooth movement. All the while those lean legs carried him forward as terrible speed.

George's legs became unstuck and he flew into the SUV. As he turned the key, the engine—he thanked God—fired immediately. George slammed the gear lever into reverse and released the handbrake. The creature let the arrow go straight for the windscreen. George flinched and ducked. There was a clunk as the arrow hit the left windscreen wiper, which came free from its mount. The arrow must have ricocheted up and hit the roof, as George heard a clack above him.

George lifted his head to look. The creature was now only two hundred metres away. Its long legs were eating up the ground, breath vaporising in the cold and streaming back from its head. It had a second arrow in the bow as George jammed down on the accelerator, spinning the wheels in a frantic scraping of rubber and flying stones.

The desert scene folded up within two seconds this time. George must have been doing forty or so when the SUV bumped across the kerb and onto the service road. He braked hard, bounced up the opposite kerb and stopped inches from the opposite building. Terrified, George looked back onto waste ground expecting to see the creature rush out of the field loosing arrows. At that range, they would surely penetrate the windscreen and kill him. Then the creature would drag him from the SUV with those long arms and tear his corpse to pieces.

But he saw only a puff of exhaust fumes fading into the night air above the waste ground, and that was all. The dark brown creature was back in the desert and George was safe on the company's site; trembling in shock, but alive.

He put the corrugated iron was back against the IT building wall before returning in the SUV to the car park. He had been gone less than thirty minutes.

George realised he had left the digital camera behind. He remembered it sitting on the bonnet of the SUV when he got the binoculars out of the car. The driver's windscreen wiper was gone as well. When the arrow had struck, it had snapped the wiper right out of its mount. It had also put a small crack in the windscreen, plus there was a minute dent and long scratch on the roof, left by the arrow's ricochet.

The damage to the car helped George convince himself that he had not dreamed or imagined what had happened. No human could ever be that lean, or that tall, or that fast. But the creature had been real. For such an advanced creature to exist on Earth, and never be reported before, was impossible. This led to only one conclusion: the desert was not on Earth.

The very thought of it made George convulse and retch. He sat in the SUV for ten minutes until he was calm enough to continue his duties.

George lived his life in a daze for the next few days. There were some comments from the other security guards, and a few questions, like was he all right or feeling ill? George made a few half-hearted apologies and waited for them all to stop their questions and leave him alone.

The idea that he had been to a different country was bizarre; the knowledge that he had been on a different planet was incomprehensible. What had happened on the triangle of waste ground? Was it the electrical building and IT area that had caused this? How in God could he be travelling through space? And why was there a change in the seasons? Maybe this desert's planet had a quicker orbit or steeper tilt. Either that, or there was an element of time travel in all this as well. The idea almost made his mind shut off.

Frustratingly, apart from the damage to the SUV and sand and gravel in the wheel treads, he could show no proof of what had happened. The camera had the photos, but that was back in the desert.

George knew he had to go back.

Not for the proof his camera could provide; digital photos could be faked and would convince no one. He had to get something on video this time. George knew he had to go back, though he shivered at the thought of seeing that dark brown creature. But this was too big to stop investigating now. This was interplanetary travel. No space ships, just instantly going from Earth to God-knows-where in seconds. When George had video, and some of that shale-like rock, plus some sand and stones for geologists to examine, he could talk about it to someone. And then his life would change, and it would be so much better.

Maybe he would go to the bosses of the company. George realised he should have thought of this before. He worked for a commercial company. What could be more commercially successful than free interplanetary travel? This was George's big chance to escape his old life; a chance like nobody else had ever been given. He saw himself being put on the board of the company in gratitude. Not that he would know what to do or anything; he would just attend meetings and vote with everyone else. The company would have to do something like that out of gratitude. And if they didn't, George told himself, it would be bad publicity for them. A few million a year in salary would be nothing to the fortune the company would make from his discovery. George could hardly sleep at night thinking about it all. His wife noticed the change and tried to find out what he was thinking about, but he shut her out. This was his discovery and he meant to make the most of it—for him.

But still the dark brown creature worried him. It was lethal. George wondered whether he should take a gun. He knew how to use one, and could borrow one. What if he had to shoot the creature to stay alive? What if that triggered an interplanetary war? No, he realised, that was ridiculous. A naked, dark brown alien with a bow was hardly from the sort of advanced civilisation that could fight interplanetary wars. That was how George thought of it after that, as a dark brown alien.

George thought a lot about it. He kept remembering those last few seconds. That incredible alien, skin dark brown and sleek, loping up the slope at George. Those bizarre elongated limbs, the compact musculature moving under the glossy skin. The hard look on the alien's face, with its overlarge eyes—a look of anger, or hunger. George couldn't say which. And the speed it could run at, it could outrun a cheetah.

George didn't have nightmares about the alien, but he certainly sweated when he thought of it catching him, those long, sinewy arms wrapping round him, snapping his spine like a twig. But he still had to go back. This was an opportunity he could not let pass by. This was unique. This was the way to fame and fortune. He had to risk all—his very life—to get it.

A few weeks later, he built up the courage to try again. George was due to be on day shifts until then, and didn't he want to try in daytime when there were more people around to notice. When the day shifts ended George had a Saturday evening shift coming up, which suited his purpose best.

This time he planned to be ultra-cautious. George would have the SUV in reverse as soon as the desert appeared. Any sign of the alien and George was out of there. This time George would have a borrowed video camera. George planned to have it mounted on the dashboard with bungee cords, recording the marvel of the passage between worlds, so that if he had to hurriedly escape he wouldn't lose this camera or his proof. If there was no sign of the alien, George would take it out and do a nice slow panning shot all the way around the foreground first, and then the same for the horizon. George hoped to recover the digital camera as well.

To wear, George had his old motorbike helmet. He hoped that would stop an arrow, although he had his doubts, but with his peripheral vision obscured, he might never see it coming. He packed it anyway. And he borrowed a gun.

It was a bolt action 5.56mm, so it fired NATO ammo. Even something as large as the dark brown alien should slow down if George hit him with one of those bullets. His friend Neil loaned him the rifle. Neil lived out on a farm and George test fired it there, twenty shots or so. George paid for the ammo, as Neal wasn't doing so well as a farmer. George also paid for another twenty rounds so he could have two loaded five round magazines and the rest handy in one pocket. The rifle came with a telescopic scope that George got Neil to remove. George had never used one and didn't need to use the rifle from a distance. He didn't want to use it all. If the alien was there when George appeared in the desert George intended to leave immediately. If George got out of the SUV to film, and the alien suddenly appeared and got close to him, he would shoot then, but only if he couldn't get in the SUV and drive off first.

As George gathered all he needed in the week leading up to the next trip to the desert it turned out to be a busy time at work. People from the IT department were messing around doing some upgrades so that there was a steady stream of IT staff and outside contractors coming and going. George wondered whether this might change things and affect the waste ground field. But a few enquiries told him it was merely improving communications between the mainframe and the numerous computers throughout the office areas. There was nothing being changed about the mainframe.

Of more concern was the timetable for the new electrical building which was being commissioned. They had been building that for some weeks and were suddenly ahead of schedule. Now the commissioning date was set for ten days time.

George did not like the sound of that. His assumption was that it was a combination of the IT mainframe computers and the electrical building that created the waste ground's special field. If the electrical building were going to close down soon nobody would be able to travel to the desert. It was now all the more important that George get video evidence to take to the bosses of the company. If he could get his evidence and show it to the bosses the company could always restore power to the building. That should get the field back.

George had a day off on the Thursday and finally had everything he needed at home hidden from his family in the garage, ready for the Saturday shift. When George came back to work on the Friday morning he found a minute examination of all video recordings going on. Mike told him that Dion had gone missing the day before. And so had his truck.

"Missing?"

"Yeah, he came back on site on the Thursday afternoon and just disappeared. He never parked it up that evening. They assumed he loaded his truck up with stuff and drove off and sold it. There was a big audit to see what's missing."

"So what's missing?"

Mike shrugged. "Nothing, except for the truck and Dion."

"So what are we doing?"

"Going over every video from 14:10 yesterday afternoon to see if we can see anything of the truck or Dion."

"Are the police involved?"

"A bit. Ronz has reported the truck missing. The cops have taken a statement. Dion's wife has been here going frantic. Apparently he should have been home last night for their kid's birthday party."

"I didn't know he had a family."

"Yeah. Well anyway we're going through the videos. You want to be in the office first?"

"No, I'll go out. Wander around a bit."

As George turned to leave, Mike handed him a memo. "Hey, take this and make sure you read it."

"Why?"

"It's a memo for all security about the commissioning of the new electrical building."

George folded the memo into in his jacket pocket as he headed for the car park at a trot. Something had happened to Dion. Something that stopped him returning. Something had gone wrong with the field. George just knew it. As the only one who knew what had happened, George had to go get him. Much as he despised Dion he couldn't leave him trapped in that desert with that alien. He might find Dion dead if he waited until his planned trip on Saturday, so he had to get him back now.

As he hurried for his SUV, George couldn't stop thinking of Dion trapped in the desert—getting worried when he couldn't return, then frantic, running the truck back and forth across the same shale rock waiting for the field to bring him home.

Once in the SUV George drove straight for the waste ground. Here he hesitated. If Dion were still parked on the rocky outcrop, there was a chance he might crash his SUV into Dion's truck. If his SUV and the truck were wrecked in a collision there'd be no hope of either of them ever getting back. There was nothing he could do except drive forward as slow as possible.

Then there was the alien. Had it turned up? Maybe Dion wasn't trapped in the desert. Maybe he was already dead with an alien arrow in his chest and the alien's hands tearing open his stomach. George retched at the thought. If he found Dion dead then the least George could do was bring his body home for the family to bury.

George realised he should have told Dion about the alien. Obviously Dion had never encountered him during his trips to the desert. If he had, he probably would not have gone back.

George cursed as he roared down the service road. All this was because Dion wanted to park up somewhere and read the paper and slack off instead of working his job full time like a normal person. George could only hope his plans for fame and a vast fortune wouldn't now be ruined by Dion's stupidity.

As soon as George saw the waste ground he knew what was wrong. The ground had been dug up, cleared of weeds and rubbish. The corrugated iron was missing from its place against the IT wall. George stopped by the kerb and got out of the SUV. It looked like somebody had rotary hoed the entire site. George still felt the air fizz in the same place as he trudged back and forth across the soft ground, his shoes becoming plastered with damp clay. But the air did not feel as fizzy as it should.

George knew he could not wait. Without the corrugated iron against the IT wall the field should be strong enough, he reasoned. The four wheeled drive and big tires of the SUV had no problems with the dug up ground. But the field didn't work. George got right up to the wooden fence at the apex and although he felt the fizzy air feeling intensify it still wasn't strong enough. George reversed back to the road and tried again, with the same results.

George realised it somehow had to be the missing corrugated iron. Apart from the dug up ground there was no other change.

George sought out Nick the gardener. Nick had a small workshop behind the transport garage. George could see the rotary hoe that he had used in one corner, still splattered in dried dirt and clay. George burst into the workshop, startling Nick. "You dug up the waste ground?" George snapped at him. "That triangular bit between the IT building and the electrical building."

"Yeah, why?"

"Why dig it up?"

"There's going to be a garden go in there. Once the old electrical building comes down there's going to be a garden and seats all through that area. It'll be a nice place for people to sit and have their morning break or lunch. It's about time this company let me clean a few of these areas up a bit."

"When did you do it?"

"What's it matter to you?"

"Please, Nick," George pleaded, "when did you dig it up?"

"Mid-afternoon yesterday. Why?"

"You didn't see a truck, one of ours, anywhere near it?" George asked hopefully.

"No, why?"

"Was there some corrugated iron there, against the wall?"

"There was all sorts of crap there. Even more came up when I dug up the ground. It's weird, that place. There's a funny feeling about it, near the middle it's almost like..."

"I don't care about that, was there a piece of green painted corrugated iron against the wall?"

"Yeah, why?"

"Please don't ask so many questions, Nick. Where's the iron now?"

"What for? It's just a piece of old iron."

"For fuck's sake," George shouted, "where's the piece of iron, you arsehole?

Nick looked shocked, but for George this was no time for politeness. "Round by the scrap metal bin near inwards goods," Nick stammered.

George whirled and headed for the doorway. Nick yelled after him, "I'll be speaking to HR about this. I'm not being sworn at like that."

George ran from the gardener's workshop. Dion had been in the desert since mid-afternoon yesterday, trapped there after Nick changed the waste ground. It all revolved around corrugated iron, like some kind of switch, though George didn't know how.

He raced round to inwards goods in the SUV. The bin placed there was for scrap metal and was emptied several times a week. Leaning over its top, George could see a large amount of metal strapping that had come from items held down on pallets. The inwards goods staff had cut this strapping off and dumped it in the bin. Below all this George could see a portion of green painted corrugated iron.

People came out of inwards goods and looked at the madman in the bin dragging out lengths of metal strapping. George cut hit hands several times before he managed to free the corrugated iron. It was slightly dented and he hoped this wouldn't affect how it worked.

But would it work? George was assuming that Nick moving it had stopped the field from working. That seemed a little too simplistic When Dion or George moved the iron away from the IT wall the field got stronger, and it lost a lot of its power when they returned the iron to its place. Now that the iron wasn't there the field should be working to its maximum and Dion should be able to return.

George imagined two scenarios. First, Dion had gone into the desert, encountered the dark brown alien was already dead. That's why he hadn't returned. Either that, or it was a problem with the field itself. George had felt that the field wasn't as strong as before. The problem had to lie with the field and the missing scrap of iron. Dion could still be alive.

George would have to try and get everything working again, then drive into the desert after Dion. He daren't simply wait for his return; the man could have wandered away from the area by now in despair and desperation.

But what if someone moved the iron again after George had left? They would both be trapped in the desert permanently.

There was a second bin nearby that took scrap cardboard and other packing materials. George dragged out a large piece that he could make a sign with. The people from inwards goods were all watching him now.

"Tony," George yelled at one of them. "Have you got a felt-tip pen? I need one urgently."

Tony looked bemused, but one of the other staff pulled a large felt-tip pen from her pocket. Snatching the pen, George ran back to the SUV and threw the cardboard and the iron into the back. He tore down the service road towards the waste ground. There was no time to worry about anyone seeing him. Mike came up on the radio twice asking what George was doing, so George turned the radio off. There was no time to go home for the rifle or camera. Dion could be dead already, or he could be alive, hiding in the cab of his truck with the alien prowling outside.

George stopped the SUV on the edge of the waste ground and stumbled across the soft earth with the corrugated iron. What was he going to do if this didn't work? George ran into the area of the fizzy feeling. He put the iron down against the IT wall in its usual place. The hairs on his body went down.

What now?

Was this like a timer switch? Perhaps when George moved the iron off to one side the field got stronger and he could travel to the desert, but after a prolonged period it reset itself.

No, that was stupid.

The thought struck him—when the corrugated iron was placed again the fence, it became a kind of focuser. George always put it in the same place, third paling from the left. And that he had copied from Dion, assuming it was a safe place to put it so that it didn't get driven over.

George lifted the iron away from the IT wall and his hairs stood up. He placed it against the third paling of the wooden fence and could feel an immediate increase in the field.

That was it.

He could see now that the field had three power strengths. Low power, which was created by the corrugated iron leaning against the IT wall and a faint feeling of fizziness in the air. Medium power, which meant no iron against the IT wall. That made hairs stand up and the fizzy feeling stronger. Move the iron across against the fence and the power went up past medium to high. And when the power was high a large vehicle could drive across the universe and into a desert on another planet.

How the hell had Dion figured all this out? George wondered whether Dion had a natural intuition about this. If George got him back alive he'd make him tell him everything.

He put the iron against the fence, grabbed the cardboard and scrawled, "SECURITY NOTICE: DO NOT MOVE THIS PIECE OF IRON," together with today's date and time. He propped the cardboard sign alongside the iron.

Back inside the SUV he slammed into gear and rolled forward, but slowly so that he wouldn't hit the back of Dion's truck on the rocky outcrop.

This time it worked.

The view of the wooden fence and the buildings rolled away and the desert took its place and enfolded him as before. He was on the rocky outcrop; Dion's truck was not there. George put on the handbrake and got out of the SUV. There was the valley. With a jolt George remembered the dark brown alien. His head swivelled frantically, looking for him, but he was nowhere in sight.

The sky seemed bright. Maybe it was midday here now. The air was cool but not as cold as the last time. Was this yet another season?

George left the SUV engine running and walked around it in a fifty metre radius, looking for some sign of Dion, or the truck, or the dark brown alien.

George found his camera where it had fallen from the bonnet of the SUV as he fled from the alien. There was also the windscreen wiper, bent in two with the arrow's impact.

Then he saw the tire tracks. They led back from the rocky outcrop and away from the shallow valley out into the desert. They were clear enough pressed into the coarse sand and stones. They were deep, with a spray of debris out to each side, as if Dion had been jamming his foot hard on the accelerator. Had he been fleeing the alien, or reversing frantically and wondering why he wasn't returning to the company's site anymore?

There was no way George was following the tracks on foot, in case the alien appeared and ran him down in an instant. He would use the SUV, but first wanted to ensure that he could bring it back to this exact spot. He needed to mark the places for the wheels.

George used his ballpoint pen for the rear left tire, pushing it down into the ground to mark the exact spot where the rear left edge of the tire met the ground. For the rear right tire, George searched his pockets and found the folded memo Mike had given him. He put that hard up against the tire, weighing it down with a stone.

Satisfied he could find the marks again, George drove forward over the rocky outcrop and down slightly into the valley to make sure he was well clear of the field, before turning the SUV round until the nose was pointing in the direction that the truck's tracks went.

George soon saw that Dion had stopped reversing after several hundred metres and had gone into a three-point turn. George followed the tracks further.

He found the truck after travelling a little over a kilometre in what looked like the long dead bed of a once great river. George saw the blue top first, rising above a dip in the landscape, and then the rest became clear as he descended the bank. There was no sign of Dion. Hoping he was asleep in the cab, George honked the horn a few times, but no one stirred.

As George covered the last fifty metres he could see the damage to the truck. There were dents in the cab as if someone had struck it with a large hammer, or thrown massive stones at it. When he got closer, George could see the windows were all smashed. Driving closer still, it was obvious some of the dents had penetrated the metalwork. What could have done that? Some sort of club or axe? The holes weren't clean edged, as George would expect with a metal axe. The alien hadn't been carrying a club or axe. Did that mean another alien had done this? How big had the alien's hands been? Was it possible he could punch through metal with a fist?

He didn't smell rot, so George hoped that Dion's corpse was not inside. Bracing himself, George reached up to the truck's door handle. The door creaked open and George was relieved to see the cab was empty.

Walking around the truck looking at the ground he could see there were obvious scuffmarks. There was a single print of a work boot in one place. That was all.

He climbed up on the truck roof and looked around. There was nothing, just rocky outcrops, sand and stones.

The truck's ignition keys were still in place. George tried them and the truck's starter whined but the engine wouldn't start. The gauges showed the fuel tank was half empty. What had happened here? Had the truck broken down or had Dion been surprised while asleep and the truck disabled later? It was impossible to say.

Back in the SUV, George couldn't decide what to do. He could drive around forever looking for Dion, or his body. Or he could go home. George wanted to go home. He was frightened, but he didn't know what to do. He felt a moral responsibility to help Dion, but he feared for his own safety.

George decided to play safe. He would go home, go to the police—that was best, he told himself. He'd convince one of them to come with him, tell them he knew where the missing truck was and that he thought Dion was dead. That should get someone's attention.

He would get them in the SUV and drive onto the waste ground and straight into the desert. No wasting time to tell them about the field and what happened. Don't give them chance to think he was mad and not believe him. Because who would believe him? George certainly wouldn't if the situation were reversed and someone told him all this bollocks about triangular shaped bits of waste ground and switches made out of corrugated iron leaning on a wall or fence.

So George would call the police, tell them he had found the truck abandoned with signs of a struggle. He'd call them from the office. When the police arrived he'd get them in the SUV, saying he'd drive them to the truck. George would drive straight onto the waste ground. The cops would freak when they found themselves in the desert but George would just drive back and forth in and out of the field until they were convinced. Then he'd point to the tracks leading to the truck.

No, he realised he'd better tell them about the dark brown alien first, warn them it was probably dangerous and they should get some guns. Would that convince them?

"Oh, to hell with it," George growled under his breath. They were the police; they knew how to handle dangerous situations. Just driving into the desert should freak them out. They would pay attention to anything George told them after that. They'd be dumb not to.

George had arrived back at the valley. He drove down the slope of the rocky outcrop then reversed carefully back between his pen and the memo and then a few metres more.

And the desert was still there.

George reversed three or more metres past that point to where the service road should be but was still in the desert. He drove back and forth twice more but nothing changed.

George was sweating as he got out of the SUV and checked where the pen and the memo were. The pen was in splinters now, the memo crushed into the ground by the tires. He had been in the right place; he could see that. There couldn't be that fine a difference that the field wouldn't work. The wheelbase for the truck and that of the SUV were different, and everything had worked before.

Somebody had moved the corrugated iron! As soon as he thought that, George realised that he couldn't feel the effervescence in the air. It had always been here around the rocky outcrop.

George realised he should have got someone to guard the corrugated iron instead of just leaving a sign.

He was stuck here.

Would someone else figure out what had happened? George knew the truth of that. There was less than one chance in a million that someone would figure this all out. He had told no one. If he had written it down then it might have been found, but he hadn't done that.

He tried to tell himself that Mike might come looking for him. Mike might have already moved the corrugated iron around and realised there was a strange feeling on the waste ground. Mike would experiment with the scrap of iron and restore the field. All he could do was hope and pray that might happen. And if it did, and the feeling returned he would be in the SUV in a flash and driving back onto the site. But when might that happen, if it ever did?

George switched off the SUV and got out. A corner of the memo was sticking out from under one of the stones. George pulled it out and smoothed it. It told him that commissioning of the new electrical building was ahead of schedule and would happen at 09:00 today. It was anticipated that there might be a brief loss of electrical power for a second or two. Security was instructed to have all gates locked open from 08:55 for ten minutes in case they failed while shut. Failures of any electrical equipment were to be reported to the site manager.

George looked at his watch: 09:21. He'd lost track of time. Nobody had moved the corrugated iron. The electrical building was dead and the field was gone forever.

George leaned against the SUV for a long while, reading and rereading the memo. He swore. He moaned. Tears welled up in his throat and he let a few sobs escape him. No one would ever know what had happened. No one was coming for him. The new electrical building would be working now and the old one would soon be demolished.

There was no going back.

There was a flicker of movement off to one side; five dark brown aliens were walking about six hundred metres away along the valley floor to George's left.

George stood mesmerised. He watched for maybe twenty seconds before one of the aliens saw the SUV. There was instant reaction as all five began running straight up the slope towards him. Two had bows and arrows. The other three seem to be carrying large stone clubs or axes—the sort of thing that could put holes in the metalwork of a truck.

George was behind the wheel of the SUV in a flash. As he raced into reverse George had the vague hope that the field would be working—just for a second. But as the SUV bounced back from the outcrop he was still in the desert.

Spinning the SUV around, George drove off at thirty kilometres per hour, steering clear of any rocks and watching for the aliens in the rear view mirror. George saw them top the rise out of the valley a few seconds later. They had already spread out as if they planned to envelope him.

George couldn't decide what to do next. He had a third of a tank of fuel. That meant about a hundred kilometres of travel across this terrain. Then what?

What he needed was a gun, or a fortress, or something.

And if he escaped the aliens, then what? *Then what?* The question kept jumping into his mind, shoving all other thoughts aside. He wasn't going back. Even if he lived through this moment, how would he survive out here? He had seen no sign of any food or water in the desert. What did the aliens live on then? Did they hunt and eat each other? George was sweating with fear and trying not to cry again. The tears would blur his vision.

He desperately wished he had never tried to help Dion, wished he had read the memo first, wished he had got someone to come with him on the second attempt. They would have seen the first alien and been instantly convinced. He wished he had never tried for fame and fortune, wished he had never been bothered about Dion hiding from work.

He crossed the riverbed. Dion's truck was off to one side as he drove. There was nothing there that could help him.

The five aliens were still following him. They ran fast. But the gap between them and the SUV had not closed, so George thought thirty was their top speed. No human had ever held a speed like that for more than a hundred metre sprint, but to them it seemed an effortless jog. They were well spread out now. If George did a U-turn to double back he would have to get past at least one of them. Even turning at a right angle, George would have to speed up to escape the outermost alien.

George saw there was something on a patch of sand just off to one side—a dead animal perhaps? Was there some other food here apart from dark brown aliens?

The corpse was mutilated and partially dismembered. It had work boots on what was left of the legs. A shredded T-shirt with what looked like the company logo on it covered the remains of the torso. Bile rose in to George's throat. He had found Dion.

He travelled another kilometre or so, the five aliens always behind him, always spread out, always keeping up. Sweat ran off him in rivers, streaming down his face, running into his eyes and stinging them. George had never been so frightened in his life. He was shaking with fear and thinking he could lose control of his bladder and bowels at any moment.

And no matter how hard he tried he couldn't see what he'd do to keep himself alive. Maybe the aliens would tire and he would escape them. *But then what?*

Something moved on a rise ahead. Two more dark brown aliens appeared out of a hollow in the ground. One had a bow. George yanked the wheel away from them. As he did an arrow passed in front of the windscreen by less than a metre. He watched the two aliens in the rear view mirror, terrified they would sprint and catch him.

Something dark was coming from his side, catching his peripheral vision. His head whipped round to see the terrifying face of an alien only metres from the SUV. His turn had driven him across the front of the five aliens and the one on the end was suddenly running alongside him. There was the dark brown skin, the oversized eyes, and a mouth open to show a bank of tiny pointed teeth on each gum. The alien's eyes were fixed on George, and he thought the alien had a look of triumph.

Frantically, George jammed a foot down on the accelerator and the SUV lurched forward. As it did the alien whirled and slammed a stone club into the passenger door behind George with a mighty crash. If he hadn't accelerated it would have been George's head.

The SUV leapt away from the alien for a few hundred metres, but crashing across several large rocks had George fearing that he would disable the car. He forced himself to slow back to thirty again. In the rear view mirror George saw the two aliens join the other five, their line extending to outflank him even more.

George kept his speed steady and drove through the desert, making sure to steer around any large rocks. He didn't know what to do or where to go. His fuel would not last forever, and although the aliens were a bit further behind him now, they showed no signs of tiring. Getting ahead of them meant little, as the SUV left clear marks for them to follow even if they lost sight of him.

George knew he couldn't reason with them. They were aliens. With a wild Earth creature he would have some idea of how not to provoke it. Wild animals understood the universal language of nature. But who knew how an alien would react? All he had seen of them was anger, or hunger, and either emotion promised him a terrible fate.

He thought to turn the SUV around and run the aliens down. He discarded the thought almost immediately. Maybe he might get one, but they were far too agile and fast for him to do better than that. And hitting a deer was enough to disable a car, he had heard. How would his SUV react to that mass of tough bone and hard sinew? And while he was stuck over the body of the one he managed to kill, the other would be piercing his body with powerful arrows and charging in with those heavy clubs held aloft.

George didn't know what to do. He didn't know what to do and there was no one coming to help him.

He had never felt as utterly alone as he did now. Even someone marooned at sea or lost in a jungle or any earthly desert had the faint hope of a human coming to their aid, a boat on the horizon or a helicopter to winch them up. But George was the only human on this planet.

As he drove carefully around the bigger rocks he tried not to look at the sinking fuel gage, willing the needle to stay at the same point. The aliens were so spread out they couldn't all be seen in the mirror and he had to swivel back and forth to see them, terrified they would suddenly break into a sprint and close in on him. They weren't tiring. They'd certainly catch up eventually, when he ran out of fuel, but he had to stave the moment off as long as he could.

Crying constantly, and frequently wailing with uncontrollable fear, George drove the SUV into the endless, alien desert, tailed by the seven dark brown figures ever on the horizon.

Made in the USA
Las Vegas, NV
24 June 2021